The Silver Reindeer

STIRLING DAVENPORT

Noth Press

Poughkeepsie, NY

DEDICATION

To Sai, for her intelligence, courage and beauty.

CHAPTER 1

From Magda Ranhubell's Journal ...

I drew the horses up to the brink of the fog which was massing over the bridge, and watched the snowflakes swirl through the mist. All was quiet, with such an eerie kind of emptiness that I felt awkward and out of place. I imagined the warmth of the Sanctuary Ddiesana, the convent I had left behind, but my mission beckoned me with greater urgency than ever.

A chill pressed into my heart through the wolf-fur lining of my coat. I had dressed in layers—a lamb's wool shirt and linen under-tunic, two pairs of woolen leggings, and plenty of rags stuffed into my fur-lined boots. My red braids were covered by an ermine hat, a gift from my father, and the only thing I had brought from home when I had entered the Sanctuary six winters ago. I pulled up my hood to hide the hat, lest someone recognize it. I had no way of knowing how long I would have to remain in the wilds, and the clouds looked storm-laden.

Both Snowdrop, my mount, and Mistral, the gray mare, were restive, pulling at my hands with outstretched necks, and snuffling at the snow with their noses. I checked my saddlebags and felt for the thick, blue blanket. I hoped it would not be missed. Everything was secure, and I pulled the dull, brown bag from inside my coat. Gently, I drew the chalice from its wrapping, and gazed at its glistening luster in the mist of snow. My fingers tingled at the power beneath the sheen of the metal.

The reindeer etched on the sparkling silver seemed to prance and lift their heads, but they no longer spoke in my mind. I told myself I could not have imagined it.

Reluctantly, I put it back, and there being no excuse to hesitate further, I let the horses have their heads. This snow was the kind we called "Little White." It would cushion their hooves as we rode up the mountain into exile. Their hoof beats were muffled in the snowy calm, soft thumps against the heavenly stillness of the fjord.

Inside the Sanctuary, there was warmth and the look of a well-swept hearth. Sister Anitra was at that moment sweeping the snow from the front doorway, and Sister Elga was wiping the last crumbs from the table. Yet for all their industry, there was a sadness tugging at their movements.

"We'd best have that sweet cider for the gathering tonight, Sister, else the High Priestess will think we've forgotten our most fundamental teachings. We must not let Her Eminence see that anything has changed." Sister Anitra finished her work, and deposited the broom in a corner by the door. Brushing off her long, blue robe and smoothing her white veil, she walked over and touched Sister Elga on the sleeve. "Sister, did you hear me?"

Sister Elga turned, and her friend saw small tears slipping down one side of her face. "I heard you, Sister, it's only that I am worried for the poor little thing. Out in this storm, with who knows how many bounty-men after her?"

Anitra shook her head. "She only just completed her apprenticeship. And why? Why did she take it?" She looked toward the ironclad panes of the window already showing the crescent of snow near the sill.

"Did she have no thought of us? Our Sanctuary will be blamed and we will never live down the dishonor." Elga's eyes were still moist.

"You are right," said Anitra. "To house the Chalice of the Silver Reindeer befalls only one out of a hundred Sanctuaries. To be the one that loses it ..."

Sister Elga was too overcome to speak.

"We must try not to worry," said Sister Anitra gently. "Pray that she'll come back, all in the Great Mother's time."

"Yes," said Sister Elga, wiping her eyes with her sleeve. "Help me bring up the cider now."

The two sisters went out, leaving the fire burning merrily as if in communication with some higher power which worried about nothing as insignificant as a young girl out in the snow with a holy vessel from a more ancient time.

From Magda Ranhubell's Journal ...

I came to a clearing a few miles from the base of the Kloedrift Mountains, and stopped to rest Snowdrop and Mistral. We were all cold, and night was only an hour away. Soon we would have to find shelter and build a small fire. I was thanking the Great Mother for the persistent fog which would hide my smoke, when Mistral neighed, and Snowdrop pranced nervously.

Turning, I saw the glint of metal through the dark trees, and realized a party of hunters approached. There was nowhere I could hide in so short a time, especially with two horses. Instinctively, I linked my hands over the place where the chalice nestled inside my coat.

I tried to count the snow-muffled footsteps in the fog, and whispered calming words to the horses. Quickly, I stuffed my ermine hat into the back of my waistband, and covered my bright hair with the plain hood of my coat. I slid off of Snowdrop and held her rein.

A rough voice emerged, though I could not find the face that owned it. "Aha! You young rascal—you won't escape us this time."

"Who do you seek?" I spoke up clearly, not wanting to be mistaken for another.

"The witch who stole the Chalice of Montrovik. Give it to us, and we'll let you go in peace back to your sisters. Or perhaps to your father, Lord Ranhubell. It's no use to deny that you carry the treasure."

I felt my heart sink to my feet, but I still fought resolutely for the courage to think. Somehow I must trick them. Great Mother forgive me for lying, I pleaded.

"What treasure? I am no priestess, nor a lord's daughter. I am leading these horses back to the others."

"What others?" the man said suspiciously. His hesitation caused several of his men to grumble, unhappy at the prospect of a cold trail.

"The hunters. Do you not know that the king's party

is out here hunting stag? Surely you must have seen them. Their camp is just over the hill."

Everyone knew King Harben's reputation with intruders. I heard muffled voices before he spoke again. "Let us see your face, then. It's dim in the fog, and we would not harm you if you are not the one we seek."

A giant shadow of a man stepped from the shelter of the snow-bound trees. As he came toward me in the darkness, I could see that he was dressed in many layers of hides and furs, and carried a sword on his belt.

I blinked in the light of his torch, and stepped closer to him. He pulled the hood from my face, roughly, holding the torch so close to me that it singed my eyelashes.

He laughed. "This is no priestess, nor I doubt even the attendant of one. And the lord who sired such a daughter would hang himself."

I shivered. Was he talking about me?

"You've a face on you, lass, that would frighten the dead—if lass you be. Come, men, we've no time to waste on false trails. There's much ground to cover tonight, and a great prize awaits us."

Before I could catch my wits, they were gone. I was both relieved and astonished at the ruffian's words, and could only stand stupidly. Far from being a beauty, I had never been called ugly before, and could not imagine what they had seen in the darkness. All I had for a mirror was the chalice. Stealthily, I drew it out and looked at myself. There I was—the same sad, blue eyes, red hair and hollow cheeks. My color was good, lips not too thin, nor chin too wide. Aside from my thinness and lack of sleep, my face was all right. Truly baffled, I put the chalice back in its pouch, and thrust it under my coat, nestled against my lamb's wool shirt.

Hearing the men speak of me as a lord's daughter reminded me of my reason for leaving home. I had not wanted to come of age. I would have been happier to have remained a child. In defiance of tradition, my father had sought to hand me Kenistar. Not many daughters ruled such large estates, unless there were no sons. My younger brother Ragnar had complained bitterly.

Kenistar. That giant, sprawling estate waiting to eat all my time and energy. And if that were not to my liking, there was our neighbor, Count Helmut of Ennaston, to whom my father planned to wed me. The nearby Sanctuary of Ddiesana had beckoned to me like a lantern of hope. Perhaps in the company of women, I could be myself.

Now, it seemed, I had closed off that possibility forever.

CHAPTER 2

Ragnar Ranhubell sat glowering over a gem-studded goblet of Vitaqua, a heavily spiced liqueur. His red-haired good looks were marred by a chronic expression of resentment, and his pale blue eyes were watery where once they had been keen. He drained the goblet and immediately refilled it from the pitcher beside him. The embossed face of the jolly inn-keeper on the pitcher seemed to leer at him.

His father stood leaning on the window sill, looking darkly out at the snow flurries dancing over the estate.

Erik Ranhubell, thirty-first Earl of Kenistar, once had red hair, too. Now it was as gray as the steel that hung on the walls of his Great Hall, though he was not yet forty winters. His eyes were the color of the lake behind his Great House, and the same shade as Magda's. By the harsh reckoning of life in Montrovik, he was old. The snow was thick on the ground now, and his daughter had left the

Sanctuary eight days before.

The Earl scowled in worried silence, fingering the notice he had found on his door that morning. "Reward ... two thousand sovereigns to the one who can return the sacred Chalice of Montrovik to King Harben... Two thousand more will be paid for the capture of the outlaw, Magda Ranhubell." Erik grimaced. "The man who posted this did not even have the courage to deliver it in person."

Ragnar said, "Nor the courage to search for her. People think the chalice has mythic powers."

The Earl snorted. "It's nothing more than a battered old silver cup with curious markings. And a priestess is nothing to be afraid of." He stepped to the window and showed his back to Ragnar. "If no one else will join me, I will find her myself."

Ragnar laughed. "She is probably on her way to sell it over the border." He took a gulp of liqueur, avoiding Erik's glowering expression. "Or perhaps she will come back home to us, looking for forgiveness."

"Here?" said Erik, with a new thought. "How well do you think the servants can be trusted? If they are found harboring her without my knowledge, I'll have their eyes burned out."

Ragnar looked up and said, "I'd like to burn *her* eyes

out. When she first left us, you said we wouldn't speak her name again in this house, that she might as well be dead. Admit it, father. You have only been waiting all this time to give her the inheritance that should be mine. She who never wanted it. Now I see how much a son is loved—how lightly a father's promises are made—"

"Watch your tongue, Ragnar. You tread on thin ice. Your sister was young and rash. I was angry. I have regretted my words many times since then, but never more than now." He balled his fists, and turned abruptly from the window to pace the room. "I should have known she had my ways—as you never have. My blood. You could show a little more concern for your sister, as you might for anyone out in this weather."

"My sister? Why should I care what happens to that selfish brat?" Ragnar bellowed. "As for the servants, they won't betray you any more than I will—though the reward is tempting, I must admit." Ragnar swayed on his feet.

The Earl said, "Your envy disgusts me. Take your drunken words elsewhere if you can't be civil."

"You call me envious, but try to remember that it has been six winters since Magda left, and it is you who have nurtured this anger in me." Having uttered the forbidden name, Ragnar pushed the cup away, suddenly feeling too restless for it, and not waiting for his father's reply, he strode from the room.

The Earl wandered to the fire and sank heavily into a high-backed, padded, oaken chair. As the logs crackled, the flames danced before his eyes, reminding him of his daughter's red-gold hair, and the tips of the flames were as blue as her eyes. What a woman she must be now. What a waste.

He glanced at the notice, and the word "outlaw" leapt out at him. He crumpled the parchment, and threw it into the fire. He had given strict orders to his men. If any tried to claim the reward, he would hunt them down himself. Even now, they might have found her—she might be on her way back to him. He clasped his left fist until the knuckles hurt.

"First a priestess—now a thief," he said to the cavernous room.

Could his daughter really be so foolish as to believe she could sell the chalice across the border for any large price?

"My foolish daughter," he mused, "foolish daughter of a foolish father ... Magda."

And he sank his head into his hands and wept.

The High Priestess Gostren of the Sanctuary of Ddiesana stood with her hands outstretched on the table. She had barely thirty-five winters, yet for all the gray in her brown braids and the sharpness of her thin, hooked nose, the bloom of girlhood still lurked in the creases of her eyes and the softness of her lips. Her piercing hazel eyes were closed and she was thinking. If she had been asked to explain her methods, she would have replied that she was asking the Great Mother for an answer, which was true in a way. But to be more precise, Gostren consorted with spirits, guardians who never failed to give her wise counsel.

The true spirituality of the Sanctuary was never more clearly seen than in the person of its High Priestess. This tradition had spanned centuries of women, wise and unwise, coming and going with the clasped hands and soft steps of devoted worshippers. It was more a feeling in the heart rather than any spoken or written dogma that promoted the choosing of a High Priestess.

There was a knock at the door.

"Yes?" said Gostren, automatically smoothing down the cuffs of her white robe and adjusting her veil.

A young woman entered. She was dressed in the light blue of a junior priestess, and nervously approached.

"Sister Hurveg, please make yourself comfortable."

Hurveg sat down in one of the leather-bottomed chairs in front of the High Priestess. She cleared her throat. "Your Eminence, I ... I had a dream."

"Ah. You have had dreams before, and I recall that the Dreams Mistress assisted you with interpretations. Is there something different this time?"

The priestess nodded. "I dreamed of the first High Priestess, Sister Hestianne Solstife."

"The one who was cast off from the tribe until she revealed her lights. This sounds like a very auspicious dream."

"Perhaps, but there is more, Your Eminence."

"Please continue."

"In the dream the High Priestess Solstife came into a snowy clearing. We were somewhere on the mountain." Hurveg held her breath, and at a nod from Gostren, continued. "So then a ball of light appeared, and it changed into ... Sister Magda."

"I see," said Gostren. She reflected on the image and found it apt. Magda Ranhubell was a bold-spirited girl who could have managed an estate like Kenistar, yet had chosen the life of a priestess.

"So was there more to the dream?"

"Well, the light was also coming from something she carried. I think it must have been the chalice. The High Priestess reached for it, but then something happened."

"What happened?" asked Gostren, striving to control her excitement.

"I do not know. Everything went black."

"Ah." Gostren made a sign of blessing. "You were wise to tell me of this dream. If you dream of this again, Sister, please see me immediately. Will you do that?"

"Oh, yes. Thank you, Your Eminence." Hurveg stood and bowed, and left the room seeming much lighter than she had when she had entered.

Gostren rose and paced the room. Magda had the chalice. And even in a dream, the High Priestess Solstife could not take it from her. What would happen when others found that only Magda could handle the artifact? This was a secret few besides even Gostren knew. But if known, Magda's life would not be worth even the bounty on her head.

The facts were bare before her, and the High Priestess returned to her chair, and sought help from her spirits.

The quiet built as the room began to fill with invisible presences whose wisdom reached tendrils in and through the High Priestess. After an indeterminate time, she opened her eyes, and laid her hands on the table. She looked at the window sill and noted how clearly the wood stood out dark against the snow. She stood and opened the window a hand's breadth to drink in the fresh, cold air.

"So. She is following a quest. I might have known it." Her heart went out to this fellow seeker, and she said, "Great Mother guide her, and help her find her way safely back to us." The High Priestess then folded her hands into her sleeves and prepared to go to Gathering.

CHAPTER 3

From Magda Ranhubell's Journal ...

It had been three days since I had been accosted by the bounty-men. I was careful to keep well off the trail, and leave as few traces of my journey as possible. Only fear kept me from laughing at the picture of them when they discovered I had slipped through their fingers so easily. And yet I was beginning to understand that the chalice was a more powerful ally than I had imagined. Even the horses were quieter, as if by some unseen hand they were calmed when I was at my most anxious.

We had camped in the hollow made by some larger boulders. It would be fairly safe, as long as no one crept up on foot. I'd had a difficult time getting Snowdrop and Mistral safely through the gap, but once inside, there was surprisingly plenty of room.

When I had made a small fire and settled in, I cooked

a small portion of grain for myself and gave the rest to the horses raw. It was all I had left of my provisions, and I knew that soon I would have to hunt like any common traveler. The thought of it sickened me, for I had grown soft, though I had enjoyed riding my father's horses and hunting before I came of age. The child's bow and arrows I had left home at Kenistar would not have helped me now, though, and I was glad there were still chokeberry trees and groundnuts if one looked for them.

Whenever I felt myself losing spirit, I took out the chalice. It always gave me a profound sense of inner strength, and I was warmed by its age-old vibrations of peace and wisdom. I could feel it like a friend, urging me toward the summit.

Tonight, I was content to sit and stare into the fire. My body was tired, and even lying down seemed a chore. I almost fell asleep with my eyes open. Just as I was slipping away, a hand gripped my neck—and I felt the edge of a cold knife on my throat.

I could not scream, though I felt the panic rise up in my throat. "Who are you?" said a cold voice behind me.

Fearing it was one of the ruffians returned, I answered, "I'm a poor servant and have been separated from the King's party. Have pity, sir."

"Liar," the man retorted, and I felt the knife tip pierce my skin. "I've just left King Harben in his tower, and by the look of you, you're no servant." He grabbed my cheek and turned my face toward him. I blinked at the firelight shining in my eyes, but I could only see that he was young and handsome, and his sleeves were lined with white fur and covered with rune marks I had never seen before.

It was clear that the chalice was not providing a disguise for me this time. In spite of the fire, I began to shiver. I tried valiantly to stop, but this only resulted in a terrible case of the hiccups.

"Oh, troll's breath," the stranger cursed, lowering his weapon, and sliding it into a worn sheath at his waist. He pulled out a persimmon, and sat on his heels beside me, ostentatiously eating, while I strove to quell my hiccups.

When at last I could breathe normally, my fears were forgotten.

The young man looked straight at me, and I was made shy once again by his well-made features and his arresting cobalt eyes that were even bluer than his cap.

"Are you ready to tell me the truth now?" he asked.

I felt an itch between my shoulder blades. I wondered why it seemed another message protruded from beneath the stranger's words.

In spite of my apprehension, I was too exhausted to match wits with him. I stared enviously at the half-eaten persimmon. The shine on the bright skin reminded me of the chalice. At the thought, a rush of strength warmed my belly, and I said, "You say I'm no servant, sir, so perhaps you will tell me what the truth is."

He fished inside his coat and pulled out a parchment, which he unrolled. He said, "Read this, Sister Magda, for no doubt this poor fire is a blaze compared with the cold grate of your cell at Ddiesana."

"It's not cold! How dare you—" I blushed, caught again, and took the parchment with shaking hands.

As the daughter of an earl, I was well-read. As I squinted at the words on the wrinkled parchment, the firelight tinted it the color of blood. My name had never been in such poor company. I started to toss the notice into the fire, but the stranger intercepted it.

I said, with all the disdain I could layer into my voice, "So, it's money you seek."

He laughed, "Do I look like a bounty-man?"

"You carry a knife," I accused.

"As any traveler alone would do," he said, indicating

the black trees that surrounded us. "No doubt, you have one yourself."

"Well, then, who are you?" I snapped, irritated that I had not added a knife to my provisions.

A wolf howled in the distance, answered by its mate. The stranger used the interruption to think, and I saw his mask drop for a moment. He seemed younger than I had thought.

When he spoke, the illusion faded. "I am Thorn, one of King Harben's magicians." He fixed his dark blue eyes upon me, and his black eyebrows seemed to take color from the trees behind him. Soft snow had begun to fall, and his hair was salted with it. I felt paralyzed by his gaze, and wondered what he searched for in my face.

At length, he must have been satisfied, because he looked away, and I let out the breath I had been holding.

"I, too, am an outlaw," he said.

CHAPTER 4

The High Priestess Gostren awoke in the middle of the night, with a feeling that something was terribly wrong. Into her mind came an image of Sister Magda. She shifted on her narrow bed, and dragged on the sheepskin robe that hung on the chair nearby. The moon shone over the snow, turning it to crystal.

Gostren was not comforted by its radiance, and as she gazed at the shimmering orb, she entreated, "Great Mother, send me counsel. I am troubled." Immediately, she had a vision—so powerful that she had to sit down, dimly aware that her robe nearly stuck to the cold wooden seat of the chair.

The vision was of a magician. He was tall and handsome, with dark curling hair and glistening blue eyes, and wore a coat with rune-embroidered sleeves. Next to him sat Magda, her face illuminated by firelight.

Gostren held her breath, and probed. What was a magician doing with Magda? Why did he seem so disturbing? Even as she asked, the face of the man transformed—became older, more determined, more … Gostren gasped. The feeling of evil was suffocating. She shivered. The image was gone, although she was sure she had recognized him. Whoever he was, he was coming closer to the girl. "Oh, Great Mother, protect her."

She lit a candle in the holder and prepared to rally the elders. They would have to perform a protective ceremony before dawn.

From Magda Ranhubell's Journal …

I doubled my saddle blanket to make a warmer seat on the frozen ground, and prepared to listen to Thorn. While I settled myself, I searched his features for signs of deceit. I wanted to be able to trust him, but I was acutely aware of the knife.

The self-proclaimed magician handed me a persimmon from his pack, and I took it, embarrassed that my hands were still shaking. The words of the priestesses came to my mind: Beware the man who puts his faith in runes. The High Priestess Gostren had told me that some magicians were dangerous men who trod on territory that was better left alone. I strove to recall the ones who had visited my father in winters past. They had been well-mannered and, to my innocent eyes, intelligent.

The persimmon was tough and sour from winter frost, but I was so involved in tasting it that I missed Thorn's first few words. As the juice ran down my chin, I picked up the thread of his story.

" ... confounded the village elders. I was reading and writing at five, ciphering at six. Mother had a friend at court, Duke Muur of Chaddis, who agreed to let me board with him, and attend a real school. I was attracted to the study of magics." He looked for my reaction, pausing to put another log on the fire.

"It's an honorable profession," I heard myself say, faintly surprised at my own words. "If I were a man, perhaps I would rather wield a birch wand than a sword."

"Well spoken. I like to look for deeper meanings, and have been told by some that I have talent."

I chewed quietly, noting an underlying bitterness in his tone. I doubted that his talent was as small as he claimed, remembering the way I had tried to hide my own abilities as a child. The clear sight and the voices on the wind were not the sort of talents approved of in my father's household either.

The stranger said no more, but looked around, as though we were being watched. It added to my unease. Firelight glinted against the snowbound trees, and Snowdrop snorted in the chill air.

I asked, "Why did you say you were an outlaw?"

"That I will tell you if you promise my words will not leave this forest."

"I promise, if you will accept that my allegiance is to the Great Mother. I will not break my vows."

He nodded. "I, too, serve the Goddess."

"Then, by all that is holy, by the Mother and the Foremother, I will not reveal your secrets without dire cause."

For the first time, I saw true respect on his face. "That is an impressive oath, and I beg you to honor it. The fate of Montrovik may depend upon it." Thorn leaned back on one elbow, and stared into the fire. "How much do you know of matters at court?"

"Very little. I have been in Sanctuary for six winters."

"And before that? As a lord's daughter?"

I shrugged. "I was not especially interested. I probably know less than a kitchen maid."

"What have you heard of the sorcerer, Master Svendal?"

I brightened. "The Great Svendal, my father called him. He is the most renowned Lore-Master in all of Montrovik, and older than any living being."

Thorn snorted, and looked away. His profile was harsh in the firelight, and I felt that I had failed some sort of test. "Renowned, yes. And skilled, without a doubt. But a villain all the same."

"You must be mistaken. Master Svendal has done many a wondrous deed. And besides, no evil can come within ten leagues of King Harben."

"You overestimate the King's priests."

"But Master Svendal has been at court since my father was a baby. Does he not perform at every ceremony of initiation and naming? And does he not soothsay and work powerful battle magics in times of war?" I found myself suddenly defending him, with the passion of a star-struck child. "It was he who decided the Battle of the Fuurthan tribes, and ended the famine in the Winter of the White Seal. He cured the entire northland of the gray wasting sickness—he cured my own father. He is a legend."

Thorn sighed and shook his head, as if I were a child and he a frustrated parent.

"You speak of the past. We have been at peace for nigh on twenty winters now, and Svendal grows weary of ceremonies and arcane study. There hasn't been a serious drought or famine in all that time. Not one flood or earthquake. And it is Svendal who urges King Harben to expand our borders. He would have us attack our peace-loving neighbor to the south."

"Queen Ederlie of Griffland?" I asked, incredulous.

"Correct."

"Impossible. Besides, Griffland is full of bogs and quicksand. No one would dare."

"Svendal dares. He has constructed huge platforms that can carry men in full armor—and their war horses. He says he will lift these with his magic, and the armies can cross the bogs unharmed."

"But surely the King does not want to fight such a war?"

"Perhaps not, but his arguments grow weaker each day, and his advisors are taking Svendal's side one by one. It is the talk of many, including some of the magicians themselves."

"Then, why did you run away? Is your voice not needed?"

"You do not understand," Thorn said, suddenly angry. He rose and began to pace.

I sat quietly. I was used to bad-tempered men, having grown up with two. I watched him warily, letting him have time to choose his words. He was a well-made man, and I found myself admiring his stride and the black of his hair against the snow. At last, he continued.

"I did everything I could to gain an audience with King Harben, but each time, I was referred to Master Svendal himself. Svendal—who has thwarted my advancement at every turning. I would get no favors from him."

The bitterness was back in his voice.

"What does he have against you?" I asked.

"Who knows? Perhaps I am less affected by his charms than others. He must know I suspect him." He gave me an oblique glance I recognized with some surprise as shyness. "And he seems to dislike my talent."

"Have you no allies at court? What about your mother's friend, that duke you mentioned?"

"Duke Muur. At first, I confided in him, but he threatened to have me arrested if I said another word against Svendal. I am only an apprentice magician, barely out of my first Forms. Such a one has few friends—and none with power."

"Well, perhaps King Harben will prevail. He has always been a wise ruler, or so they say."

Thorn shook his head. "One moment, he appears strong and purposeful, with a smile for everyone. Then, he acts as one entranced. I believe Svendal works magic upon him—and others. No one suspects the magician for the very reason you so eloquently stated: he is a legend. If you disbelieve me, consider this." He squatted and lowered his voice. "He has twice tried to have me killed."

Thorn unrolled his rune-covered sleeve and showed me a serpentine white scar that disappeared above the crook of his elbow.

"How – how did you get that?"

He shook his head, covering his arm again. "White fire. He thought me bound but I escaped."

CHAPTER 5

From Magda Ranhubell's Journal ...

I weighed Thorn's words, and for the first time, wondered if he might be mad. So he'd been wounded by magic, but perhaps that was common. Was it possible he alone had seen through the plans of the most powerful magician in our kingdom? Could the famous Svendal be in favor of a war? And why would he want to kill a poor apprentice like Thorn?

"You don't believe me. Fine. Only remember your promise." Abruptly, he rose and lifted his pack in one fluid motion, and I scrambled to my feet, following an impulse I vaguely understood.

"Wait," I urged. "I do not think you are lying."

"Are you certain?" he said, sarcastically.

"I believe the Great Mother has guided you to me." My cheeks felt warm. "Please, forgive my hesitation. I, too, am

in danger."

"Yes." *He folded his arms, still standing, and fixed his dark eyes upon me.* *"Why did you steal the chalice?"*

"I cannot explain," I said, truthfully. I wished he had not asked, and felt a deep uneasiness about the whole subject. When I tried to remember my action, my mind was empty. I remembered the silence of the chamber where the chalice had been kept at the Sanctuary, the innermost room in the building, and the one where a priestess was most likely to be left alone in meditation. I remembered the compulsion that had come over me, and the certainty that the chalice had spoken to me—somehow—but it was as if my memory was a cloud blown across the surface of the moon.

The High Priestess had once drawn me aside and said, "Sister, I notice that when you are in meditation, you seem to go farther than the rest of us. You should start the deep training before another winter has passed." Perhaps that would have helped.

"Whatever your reason, you have a price on your head," said Thorn. "In that, we are united. For as long as I'm alive, Svendal does not sleep well. If you wish, I will be your protector until we reach the other side of this forest. But let us pledge now to be open with one another."

"Agreed."

Thorn sat down again, propping himself against his pack.

Feeling brave, I said, "Since we are being honest, tell me, were you bound for Griffland when you saw my camp fire?"

"Yes. Queen Ederlie has magicians of her own. Perhaps together they can defeat Svendal's magic—and thus avert a war. As outlaws, we will have to put our case most eloquently."

We, he had said. The full realization of my plight silenced me. I was glad that my new companion had taken my acquiescence for granted, and did not point out that I had not said which way I was headed. I was not sure how he would view my reliance on intuition, but I was too tired to think about it, and sleep plucked at my eyelids.

Just then, an owl hooted, one long and two short notes. Thorn was transformed. He sat on his heels, as if in deep contemplation, his eyes closed, and when he opened them at last, they were glazed as with a fog. Blinking as if nothing had occurred, he leaned forward to stir the fire, causing a glowing spray of wood chips to fly and fall like miniature stars.

I pondered what I had overheard of magicians from my father, that they earned power and long life by giving up the ambitions and pleasures of ordinary folk. In that, we were similar. But there was something else I remembered. Each of them was connected to a particular animal or tree. Feeling bold, I asked, "Was that owl your special friend?"

He looked at me for a long time, his eyes intense. "My Keeper, yes."

"Keeper?"

"Very early in our training, we are bonded to a particular plant or animal or bird. We call this spirit our Keeper."

"Why?"

"The Keeper negotiates for us with the Powers. The Powers of Light and Darkness. Then the Keeper pays the price for such a favor."

"What price?"

"In small matters, a feather or bit of fur or twig left in a sacred place. But there are times when an event is so momentous that a very large favor or special talent is needed. A flood or a plague will demand a sterner price. Then, with all the proper covenants and seals, the animal or tree is sacrificed."

"Sacrificed," I said, horrified.

I could see that Thorn was regretting his candor by the nervous way he stirred the fire, as if he were angry with both it and me. "You are a strange girl. You cause me to speak of things I should not."

"But we agreed to be open with one another, did we not?"

"Yes."

"Then explain this sacrifice to me," I said.

"If the sacrifice is not made, the magician forfeits not only his power, but his life. It is part of the covenant between the magician and his Keeper."

I began to feel a sense of deep foreboding. "And what is Svendal's Keeper?"

Thorn fixed me with a meaningful gaze. "No one knows." He lifted his head, and his eyes swept the glen. "It is the secret of his power. I have asked myself many times these last few moons what caused the death of this man's reindeer or that one's child—"

"Child." I gasped and stared at Thorn. What manner of man would bond with such a Keeper?

Thorn shook his head, as if to clear it. "I do not welcome such thoughts, but it seems to be my gift to have them."

I shivered, feeling as Thorn did, that we were being watched—by Svendal or the bounty-men. I was not sure now whom I feared more.

When Magda was asleep, Thorn watched over her, and pondered her quest. Asleep in her blanket, she seemed little more than an innocent child with her soft, ruddy cheeks and bright braids peeping out from beneath the ermine hat.

He closed his eyes and pictured his Keeper, the great owl who was his spirit guide. In moments, the witching darkness was pierced by two glowing eyes in the notch of a pine across the glen.

"Nanitma," he called softly, speaking the owl's secret name.

The owl flew down, its feathers barely ruffling the air, and landed at Thorn's feet. With supreme dignity, it raised and lowered its tufted ears. One downy feather fluttered slowly to the ground, and Thorn picked it up carefully.

"Thank you, my friend," he said.

From Magda Ranhubell's Journal ...

I awoke just before dawn to the falling of soft snow. I had the strong impression that I had heard a sound—like the snapping of a twig. I looked for Thorn, who had fallen asleep sitting against the bole of a pine, hunched within his fur-lined coat, his dark head barely showing beneath his blue cap. The branches sheltered him from the falling snow, so I decided not to wake him.

I shook the powdery flakes off my blanket, nervously watching the trees. The bears might be in hibernation, but the wolves were not. I was still haunted by last night's conversation, and moved quickly through my ablutions, flinching at the slightest sound.

For all my skittishness, I was glad that Thorn was asleep. Though I might be an outlaw, I was still a priestess. It was time for First Light Meditation.

I found a clearing where I could see the spires of the Kloedrift Mountains through the trees, and swept clean a patch of ground to stand in. Then I crossed my hands over my breasts and fixed my eyes on the lofty sight. Quietly, to myself, I recited the words of thanks for First Light: "Oh, Mother, Creator, thank you for giving us your candle to light our way. May our actions bring you honor and joy this day." It was the custom to add one's own request here.

"Oh, Great Mother," I whispered, "Protect me—and my companion—in this blessed wood that has stood here many

winters." I breathed in the scent of the pines, and felt the benevolence of the trees around me. As always, the ritual gave me comfort.

How could magicians rely on the powers of light and darkness, I thought? How much better to put trust in the Great Mother. I realized that I had digressed from my concentration, a thing no priestess should do.

"Forgive me, Great Mother," I started again. I closed my eyes, and took a deep breath, but try as I might, I could not still my mind. I took off my woolen mittens, and blew on my hands. My stomach rumbled with hunger, and I chided myself for letting such matters distract me. Yet, I knew this was not the cause of my unrest. I could not rid myself of the feeling that I was being watched.

Blinking snow from my eyelashes, I searched the area for signs of an intruder. Gradually, I became aware of a dark shape in the tree above me.

It had the outline of a hawk or owl—only much bigger. My teeth began to chatter, and I almost called out to Thorn when suddenly the bird—if bird it was—disappeared.

I could not remember when the snow had stopped falling. Thorn lay still, his blanketed form covered by a thin layer of white that had filtered through the branches above. The air was still bitter cold, and I cupped my frozen hands around my nose and blew my warm breath into the hollow. It helped a little, but did nothing to quell my nervousness.

Drawn by that same motivation that had started me on my quest, I reached under my coat for the bag, and drew out the chalice.

Its silvery luster seemed magical in the predawn haze, and the reindeers carved into its surface pranced and danced without moving a hoof. I shivered with new energy, elated that I had come this far. I had eluded the bounty-men and even managed to find a friend. Whatever the peril ahead, I would be devoted.

Feeling reassured, I slipped the chalice back into its pouch, folded my hands again, and begged, from my heart. "Great Mother, who resides in the heartbeat of the raven and the blood of the stag, in the breath of the wind and the caress of the dawn light, from that vastness of love where you live, please guide and watch over us ... "

A twig snapped again, and I opened my eyes. I don't know how long I stood, paralyzed by my own fear, listening to every creaking branch, every whistle of the wind.

For some reason, I was reminded of Thorn's warning about Svendal. Through the curtain of swirling white, the trees looked like dark sentinels. One of them moved.

I gasped. There stood a tall, bearded man in a long,

dark cloak and high hat. His black eyes bored into me like coals, and his form was like mist. I started to cry out, when the figure disappeared. From the corner of my eye, I thought I saw a bird flapping off into the clouds. Thorn's owl—or another? I stood up, brushed snow off my woolen breeches, and scanned the trees. The glen looked empty. Too empty.

Suddenly I knew what was missing—the horses.

"Thorn," I cried. "Wake up."

CHAPTER 6

Erik Ranhubell reined in his stallion at the rise of the hill leading to the Great Keep of Montrovik, King Harben's stronghold. The dark gray snorted in the wintry air, sweat freezing on its withers.

Erik ran a hand through his own gray hair, which was damp with both sweat and snow. King Harben's order had been curt. It was clear that the Earl of Kenistar had no choice but to present himself as soon as possible.

His son Ragnar joined him moments later, accompanied by six manservants mounted on famous Kenistar mares. These large, dappled grays had big, spatulate hooves and wide rumps, bred for work and war on the craggy highlands of the Earl's estate.

"Bless your fingers and toes, Father," said Ragnar, giving the traditional Kenistar greeting.

"And yours," said the Earl.

Ragnar had been about to say more, but was struck silent by the magnificent view. The Great Keep sprawled possessively over the valley. Icicles decorated the stone turrets, and groves of pine stretched thickly on every side, as if hiding the stronghold from the eyes of the curious. Branches heavy with snow glistened in the winter light. Plumes of smoke could be seen rising from various parts of the keep, and he could imagine the welcoming aroma. A deep ravine around the Keep further protected it from wolves and other predators, and spanning the ravine was a drawbridge large enough to accommodate a small army.

Beyond the Keep herds of reindeer in the distance made their way toward grazing lands to the south, past fences bent nearly over with heavy clouds of snow.

Ragnar glanced surreptitiously at his father, curious as to the wording of the King's message. It was obvious that the Earl had been summoned to account for Magda's actions. This could bode well for Ragnar, if he kept his wits about him.

"Do you think the King will ask for your title and lands?"

With a hard stare at his son, Erik nudged his horse's flanks, and with a snort, the animal began to descend the steep hill. Erik was in no mood to deal with Ragnar's ambition.

When the small party reached the edge of the ravine, a guard called out for them to state their business.

The Earl said, "I am Lord Erik Ranhubell, thirty-first Earl of Kenistar." He held up the King's letter, which bore the distinctive red seal with two crossed reindeer's horns.

"You are expected," called the guard. With a massive creaking, the drawbridge was lowered into place. The horses clopped over it eagerly, their hooves a merry sound in contrast to the beating of Erik's heart.

Once inside, his nervousness was somewhat soothed. The King's minister, Lürgen Floss, greeted him warmly, saw that the Earl's horses were well-stabled, and invited the entire company to a hearty repast in the small dining room reserved for guests.

With a good meal in his belly, a glass of mead by his hand, and a warm fire crackling on the hearth, it was difficult for the Earl to feel any presentiment of danger. It was a mild shock when Minister Floss reappeared and announced, "The King will see you now."

Ragnar's heart beat faster, and he rose when his father did, but Lord Floss said, "Only the Earl's presence is required, young man."

Ragnar sat back down, masking his elation. He liked it here—good food, good drink ... He winked at the pretty servant who refilled his glass, recalling tales of the ease with which one could acquire a bed companion at King Harben's court.

Several glasses later, Ragnar sat alone before the dying fire in the dining room hearth.

He did not notice when someone else came into the room, a man dressed in dark velvet and mink. This man sat in the corner, toying with a glass from which he never took a sip, and his long-nosed face bore the craft of a weasel as he watched Ragnar from the shadows and stroked the silk of his black beard.

Finally, he approached, and said, "Why, Ragnar. It's good to see you again. You have journeyed long and must be tired. Hurry, girl—fetch Lord Ragnar another mead."

"Do I know you, Sir?" asked Ragnar, blinking to keep the man in focus.

"I am Svendal, and you last saw me when you were a babe in your mother's arms."

Ragnar's eyes stung with tears. "You knew my mother?" The famous name of the Master barely registered.

"Yes," said Svendal. "It was she who begged me to come and cure your father of the wasting sickness." He narrowed his coal-black eyes at Ragnar, then said, "It is too bad she did not tell me of her own trouble. I might have saved her, too."

Ragnar sniffled. "I wish I could remember more of her. She died when I was in the cradle. My sister was but three winters older."

"Your sister ... Magda."

"The brat," said Ragnar, raising a defiant chin.

"Ah," said Svendal, "we are of one mind there."

"I would sooner claim kinship with a snake," Ragnar blurted, with a gesture that toppled his flagon. Ruefully, he watched the trickle of mead that beaded the table.

"True, she has done a terrible thing," said Svendal, drawing his finger through the same thread of mead. "Stealing the most treasured prize in all Montrovik—the Chalice of the Silver Reindeer."

"Oh, that is only her latest trick. She has never cared for anyone but herself. No doubt, when she is caught, she will have some tale of being told by a bear to do it—or she will have taken it to perform some dark ceremony in the woods."

Svendal's smile was hidden in his beard. "Then, you know she is in the woods?"

"Well, of course."

"But, exactly which woods?"

Ragnar only stared.

"Would you like to know where she is?" asked Svendal.

"By the King's ale, I would."

"Well, it so happens that I do know her whereabouts, and I have been asking myself, how can I use this information to my best advantage?"

Ragnar's eyes lit up. "Tell me. I will go and bring her in myself."

Svendal cocked his head. "Why should I tell you and let you win the reward? What will you give me in return?"

Ragnar said, feeling rash with drink, "I will perform an equal service for you. Ask anything of me."

"Are you certain?"

"Ask and it shall be done," Ragnar said, slurring his speech. But his gaze was cold and unwavering.

"Well," said Svendal, "there is a certain young man who has broken his oath as a magician, and who has indeed brought disgrace upon all magicians. Knowing that he would have to face me and take the consequences of his rebellion, he has instead run away. He and your sister are together. I want you to apprehend him." Svendal pulled a small pouch from his pocket, and poured its contents on the wooden table. Bright sovereigns gleamed in the lamp light. "Take what you need to buy supplies and help. There are many in the King's army who can be hired for the right price."

Ragnar raised an eyebrow, and cupped his hand around the gold. "And who is this young man?"

"His name is Thorn. Thorn Litvar of Traenna."

"By all that's holy, I will bring him to you, Master Svendal. Only tell me which way have they gone."

"To the south. Here—take this talisman. It will help you to find their trail." Svendal handed Ragnar a whitened piece of bone.

Ragnar turned it over in his hand. "Deer?"

"That is of no importance," said the sorcerer. "When you have returned, I will see that you are rewarded with a title and lands of your own. Long have you been deprived of your inheritance, Ragnar of Kenistar."

Ragnar's ruddy face gleamed, but he said, "What of my sister?"

"She will meet a suitable fate, have no fear."

While the rest of the castle slumbered within the ancient keepstones of Montrovik, a sinister shadow moved back and forth in the flickering candlelight of the sorcerer's tower rooms.

A moment later, the candles in the tower were extinguished, and this same shadow emanated from the window like a sigh, and launched itself onto the chill night wind.

CHAPTER 7

From Magda Ranhubell's Journal ...

Hastily, I gathered my blankets together and stumbled over to wake Thorn. He was in a heavy sleep, and I had trouble rousing him.

When I told him what had happened, he was angry.

"Powers of Darkness," he cursed, as he bundled his gear together with a noisy abandon that cared nothing for the usual woods-silence.

I sensed that his anger was mostly directed at himself for sleeping through the incident, but I nonetheless watched him carefully.

The only men I had known well were my father and brother. My brother's rages always ended in violence, and my father's dark humors could last for days.

At home, I had been used to making myself scarce before I became the target of their anger. Now I looked at Thorn. His face was red, his forehead puckered, and he muttered more curses, fairly spitting. If he'd had a cup of Vitaqua in his hand, he would have been right in style with Ragnar. I determined to be on my guard as I picked my way over to gather my pack.

Thorn paid me no attention. He knelt, muttering, near the bare patch of ground where my pallet had been. In spite of my fear, I was curious and came closer.

"Ssh," he hissed.

I waited, feeling the first snowflake of the morning wet my cheek. Perhaps he was meditating, although from our earlier conversation, I could not be sure. I missed Snowdrop and Mistral, wondering if they had found their way home, or if they were being tended by whatever thieves had taken them.

Thorn knelt, as still as a tree. Guiltily, I remembered that I had not completed my First Light Meditation, and I forced myself to focus my eyes on the highest peak of the Kloedrift Mountains.

A few minutes later, I finished my mental recitation, feeling much better. I saw that Thorn had arisen, and was brushing icy particles of earth from his knees.

"We're being followed," he said, destroying my new calm. "And not just by the man you saw."

"You mean that bird I told you of?"

"That was not a bird, but one of Svendal's makings. A thing sent to watch us—then return and report." Thorn stared into the pre-dawn gloom among the trees. "Or it may have been Svendal himself."

"He has the power to change shape, then? I had heard of this."

Thorn nodded, looking worried. "It's a great magic, one I have not mastered. To do it, one must be with one's Keeper a long time. It takes much faith."

I held my arms out from my sides. "I wonder how it would feel," I mused, "to have a set of wings and talons for feet."

Thorn snorted. "You will never know." He looked as if he were seeing something in his mind. "We are being followed by someone else, though. No bird steals horses."

"Who are they?" I whispered.

"I'm not sure. I don't recognize the signature."

"Signature?" I flushed, feeling at a disadvantage.

"Every living being, whether of earth, air, water or

stone, has a signature. Then there those beings from worlds beyond, and their signatures are quite distinctive."

I sniffed to myself. Magicians. The lore was clear. There was earth and there was the land of the Mother. All else was a mystery better left alone.

Thorn ignored my silence. "The tracker is human, I think. But I can feel Svendal's mind very close to him. I feel sorry for the poor fool when his job is finished."

I wrapped the blanket over my shoulders for warmth. With one last look around, Thorn tossed his belongings on his back, and forged into the lead. He carries his anger well, I thought. Whatever his feelings, he has better manners than my brother.

Soon we were plunging through the drifted snow between the dark, frozen trees, while the wan rays of dawn blinked in and out. It was slow going without the horses, and we saw fewer pines. More and more, the terrain was thick with the gnarled cedars unique to the Kloedrift Mountains.

Several times that morning, a shadow fell over us. Once I looked up to find its source, fearing it would be the ominous bird again, but I was unable to catch a glimpse before it disappeared. If Thorn was aware of it, he said nothing.

By mid-afternoon, I could hardly keep my eyes open. I called to Thorn.

He turned and came to my side. "What's wrong?"

"I cannot go another step."

Seeing my exhaustion, he squinted at the pale sun. "All right. No doubt your life in the cloister has spoiled you for any hardship."

His insult barely registered, as I slid the pack from my shoulders. In doing so, the bag that held the chalice came loose from inside my coat. The sacred relic fell into the snow, where it made a faint bong against the stone-hard ground.

I caught my breath and glanced at Thorn, appalled at the way his eyes glittered at the sight of the chalice. Before I could stoop to retrieve it, he had stretched his long fingers to grasp the handles on either side.

"Ouch," he cried, sucking his fingers. Where they had touched the silver, there were white patches of burnt flesh. He stared at me with astonishment. "What are you, that you can touch this thing?"

"I am a priestess," I said with more dignity than I felt, putting the precious object into my bag and pulling the cord tightly. I did not stop to wonder why it had burned Thorn. I was upset with myself for dropping it, and irritable from lack *of food or rest.*

I moved toward a bare spot of ground in the lea of a pine while Thorn packed his hands with snow and mumbled some sort of incantation. He buried a piece of his precious food, and I remembered what he had said about offerings to his Keeper. I could sense an ensuing fight between us, and wished to be asleep before it erupted.

I had barely spread my blanket before Thorn was beside me, holding my arm.

"Tell me all you know about the chalice—hold back nothing," he ordered.

The steel in his voice reminded me of the knife he carried.

I looked around wildly. This was no place to impart secrets—automatically, I looked up expecting a shadowy form to be watching.

"Not here," I whispered.

"Where, then?"

"A wild, protected place—perhaps a bear's cave or a lair blessed by wolves—"

"You are daft, priestess. Your superstition wastes time. I need to know the properties of the chalice—now."

"Listen to me," I said, trying to pry his hand from my arm. "We cannot expose the chalice to danger."

"And yet it shall be protected by bears and wolves? You are mad."

"It is not safe here," I shouted. "Please, Thorn, you must believe me." My voice quivered, and I stopped, ashamed. I had been on the brink of begging him for help. What business did I have with this magician? I was a priestess of Ddiesana.

I said, "I know not why the chalice has chosen me. But remember, it is an ancient thing—the foremothers say it was brought to us by the reindeer themselves. It is a thing of the land, not of shrines and palaces. Kill me if you must, but I will not betray its trust."

Perhaps this showed in my face, for Thorn's next words were gentle.

"It's cold—you'd better rest."

He turned away, and I must have sunk swiftly into sleep, for next I knew, it was moonrise.

CHAPTER 8

Erik Ranhubell had not spoken with King Harben since the King's last tour of Kenistar some winters ago. The Earl muttered to himself all the way up the stone stairway that led to the uppermost audience tower.

"She's only a daughter, after all ... not my heir," he huffed and puffed as he climbed. "Besides, she wasn't under my roof when she took it. If she had been, I'd have tanned her hide 'til she glowed," he swore. "Reindeer balls," he grunted, adjusting his vest over his well-muscled chest and stroking his gray beard, "I have nothing to be ashamed of."

He had reached the top of the stairs, and two guards came forward, impeccably dressed in uniforms that made Erik long for past days in the King's army.

They led him into a small throne-room, and the Earl saw that King Harben sat facing a large fireplace, a table at his left hand and an empty chair flanking him on the right.

Erik coughed discreetly, and the King turned.

"Come in, my friend. Welcome to my court. It was good of you to make such speed."

Erik bowed, drew his sword, and held it out to the King, hilt first.

"Put your sword away, General. We have no need of formality between battle mates."

The use of his old title warmed Erik's heart, but, under the circumstances, he was wary of such intimacy. The Battle of the Crags was long past.

The King was beaming at him, and Erik felt tongue-tied. Was he expected to begin? What an alarming prospect.

"Your Highness—" he croaked, and cleared his throat again.

King Harben laughed softly, and shook his head. "Forgive me if I have made you uncomfortable, old friend. But these are troubling times." He fixed his eyes on Erik, "And I must ask, what are you doing about this daughter of yours? You know that when we find her, I must deal with her harshly."

"Sire, I speak as a father," said Erik, choosing his words like a wolf stepping on an icy pond. "I have had my men scouring our lands and the forests nearby. There has been no sign of her. If you had not called me hence, I meant to go myself, and make a wider search."

"I see," said Harben, bringing his goblet to his lips, but his eyes remained fixed on Erik.

"What more can I do?" asked Erik, unnerved by the King's stare.

Harben sighed. "Consider this."

A feeling of dread entered the Earl like a cold wind.

"Your daughter has stolen a priceless relic, an artifact that belongs to all of Montrovik—not just the priestesses who guard it."

Erik nodded, miserably.

"What is not widely known is that the Chalice of the Silver Reindeer bestows a power—a power which lets me rule."

"But—you are King. What greater power is there?"

"In Montrovik, it is not enough to be King. One must have the blessing of the chalice. For in it resides the spirit of the people and the light that keeps the trolls and demons underground."

Erik reddened. "Sire, my grandmother told such tales. Surely, you don't believe—"

"There are many things beyond our control," said Harben in a voice like iron.

Erik swallowed. "Then, what of your magical advisors, Sire? What of Master Svendal?"

The King grew pale, and he looked over his shoulder. "Svendal, yes, he could help ... still, I wanted to give you the chance to find her first. You are her father. It is your blood that runs in her veins."

Erik fell to one knee, and said, "Upon my oath of fealty, Sire, I vow that I will bring the chalice safely to you."

A spark of hope entered the King's eye, but it was extinguished by a cold wind that flew in the door. Master Svendal's tall figure entered and approached the fire.

"Well, if it isn't the Earl of Kenistar," said the sorcerer.

Erik rose to his feet and bowed. "Master Svendal. It is good to see you again. A day doesn't pass that I don't thank you for curing me of the wasting sickness."

"Sit down," said Svendal, and his voice carried an

authority that put King Harben's to shame. Svendal snapped his fingers, and a tall chair magically appeared between the King and Earl. He lowered himself into it, looking back and forth between the two.

"So, Your Majesty, what has this worm promised you to save his skin?"

"Worm?" started Erik.

The King waved him to silence and said, "The Earl is pledged to find her, Master Svendal. There's no need to insult him. He's a loyal subject, as are you."

"Is he?" sneered Svendal. "And how loyal was he when he allowed his daughter to ride and hunt all over Kenistar—when he should have been preparing her to wed his neighbor, the Count of Ennaston. Perhaps I should not have spared his life."

"I had lost a wife. I was a doting father, I know," blustered Erik, rising to his feet. "Of course, I taught her to hunt, and she had such a hand for it, too." He stopped at the look on Harben's face, and the sneer on Svendal's.

"You are right, Svendal," said the King. "He is a rebel. Perhaps I should have added his name to the notice."

"But, Sire—" The King's expression silenced Erik. All

trace of friendship had vanished.

Svendal's teeth gleamed white in the firelight, and his smile was a grimace. Erik was struck with a dark suspicion. He raised his eyes to the sorcerer.

"What would you have me do, then, oh wise one?"

"Do not mock me, worm," said Svendal. "Find the witchling and bring the chalice here, or you will never see your dear child again."

"What do you mean?" demanded Erik, rising to his feet.

"I could destroy her with a wave of my hand, but I am giving you the opportunity as a loving father to find her first, and restore the treasure to me—and to our beloved King."

The Earl looked at King Harben, whose features were frozen into the mask of a stranger. Gone was the shining hero king who could stir any soldier to throw down his life. It was painful to see what he had become.

Avoiding Svendal's stare, Erik bowed again. "I will find her. I have sworn it, my Lords."

When he had left the room, Erik hurried down the stairs, his boots clattering on the cold stones. He raced to the suite of rooms he and Ragnar had been given.

"Ragnar. Come here to me."

"Lord Ragnar has left the Keep," said a servant.

"Where did he go?" bellowed Erik.

"He did not say," said the boy, and scurried off, carrying a stack of soiled bed-linens.

Feeling older than the shields that lined the King's Great Hall, the Earl collected his small party, procured some fresh stores and blankets from the King Harben's warehouses, and set out into the forests.

"Which way are we bound, my Lord?" asked one of his men.

"To the south," said the Earl, "for my daughter is a creature of sun and light." Patting his horse, he led the party into the thick forest that reached gnarled fingers toward the peaks of the snow-capped Kloedrift Mountains.

Far ahead, Ragnar rode, holding the whitened bone in his left hand, his sword in his right. The talisman gleamed in the moonlight, and, as Svendal had predicted, it glowed red on one end like a beacon. As the young man fixed on his goal, the petulance in his face dissolved, and the mask of the warrior began to emerge. The rough men who rode with him were primed for the chase, used to hunting bear and weasel. This was better.

CHAPTER 9

Svendal woke and stepped down from his four-posted, walnut bed onto a soft layer of wool carpets. He dabbed cold water onto his face from a golden ewer, and groomed his long beard with a small-toothed, ivory comb.

The sorcerer's apartments were luxurious, even by court standards, although they had once been the austere chambers of a young appointee. Svendal had attained his post long before others twice his age with only half his talent. Perhaps his defects of character had given him an edge, since he was unencumbered by matters of conscience.

Winter after winter, as his proficiency grew, he was the recipient of lavish gifts. Not only was King Harben generous, but many a lord sought favors. Thus, as Svendal's wealth increased, he developed a fondness for beautiful things, and not only for their beauty. He felt their power, for, as any practitioner of magic knew, they were alive.

When he sat in the carved oaken chair each morning, he felt the spirit of the old tree that had fallen in the forest, its sap preserved under a crust of ice. His silky bed comforter shimmered before his magical gaze as if it still warmed the back of a strong, black mountain goat. The silver brooch on his cloak was a glistening river of moonlight that spoke to him in the ancient tongue of metals.

Each of these living beings around him offered a precious elixir from which Svendal drank the nectar of rejuvenation. No one would see the lines etched into his face nor the withering of his body from the prolonged use of magic. If these living agents suffered in the process, Svendal had no room for scruples. He had other worries—and had done worse crimes.

This morning, he composed himself, his hands around a quivering bundle on the oaken table before him. He focused his attention inward. An oppressive quiet permeated the room, and with it a foul stench, which Svendal ignored.

Fingers laced together to form an intricate symbol, the sorcerer intoned, "Master Odowendus of the Underearth, I, Svendal, humbly request your presence."

The room was smothered under an immense cape of darkness, from which not a chink of light escaped. A cry issued from every corner of the room, a loathsome sound that announced the entrance of the Keeper. A whimper came from the bundle.

Half human and half monster, Odowendus appeared perched on the bedstead, surrounded by a sickly halo, a gray pall that illuminated nothing else. The Keeper's huge, misshapen body was a greenish mass of pustules and scars, its features barely recognizable.

From the safety of the darkness, Svendal's lip curled with revulsion, but his voice was controlled.

"My master, I greet you. I, your servant, beg of you to grant me another sight of my enemies—and of my prize."

As he said these words, he unwrapped the bundle, revealing a dazed and blinking human infant. Svendal's hands twitched at a memory—a baffled midwife's face—a loose end he would have to attend to.

The creature on the bedstead spoke, and its voice was a silken tenor fashioned from the souls that fed it. "I will gladly take this morsel, but let me remind you, sorcerer, that I will need another before the next full moon. The soul of the last creature you sent me no longer burns. I grow hungry."

The child, having gotten its breath at last, squalled and kicked his arms and legs. Svendal smothered the infant's mouth with his long-fingered white hands.

"I understand and obey, Master. Even now I am preparing to serve you not one but an army of souls." He thought of how King Harben and his loyal men would be swallowed by the bogs of Griffland when he removed the magic from the platforms.

"Splendid," said Odowendus. "You will be suitably rewarded."

Svendal's eyes glittered in the darkness, and his hands clenched. "Show me. Please."

In an instant, a dazzling image appeared to him. The baby's muffled screech was a distant sound, as before him swirled a cloud of snowflakes. Two humans with packs upon their backs ascended a steep incline dotted with dark trees whose gnarled and grasping branches were burdened with snow. He frowned. Why did the travelers show no signs of frostbite or fatigue?

"The chalice," he whispered.

The swirl of white disappeared as swiftly as it had come. When he opened his eyes, the Keeper and the bundle were gone, and dawn's light crept into the chamber.

Svendal blinked, feeling a residue of supernatural strength suffuse his body. His bony chest swelled with the taste of the power that would be his one day. His fist closed upon itself as he imagined it closing upon the chalice.

A knock sounded on the door, and Svendal frowned. Then he clapped his hands. Immediately, the door swung noiselessly inward on its wooden hinges. A young servant appeared with a breakfast tray, which she deposited without a word, fingers trembling, eyes downcast. Svendal barely noticed her presence, and the servant scurried from sight without showing her back to the sorcerer.

After a perfect omelet of sparrowhawk eggs, a half-pitcher of winter grape juice, and a flaky crust of barley bread, Svendal covered his fine linens with a wool tunic and leggings, donned a closely woven, rune-embroidered cloak, and pulled on thick hide boots. Last, he placed a tall hat upon his long, black hair.

He gazed sternly upon the fire burning merrily in the hearth, and it leapt up, then dwindled to an ember.

He took one more look at the opulent room, which seemed cowed by his very presence, and his deft hands wove the usual protection on his door with hardly an effort. Like so many of his powers, it was a habit.

In minutes, he had descended the curved stairs, and

entered the courtyard by the armory. He nodded with satisfaction at the workers engaged in the construction of a large, wooden platform. When this was completed, it would serve as a model for others like it. Then he would empower the platforms with magic enough to carry an army to the swamps of Griffland.

I will draw the runes with a stag's blood, he thought. He smiled as he imagined how he would spill that same stag's blood on the ground, watching those very platforms fall like dead leaves into the quicksand. Odowendus would be pleased.

Ironically, Svendal had forgotten that a stag had once been his Keeper. If asked, he would not have been able to say when he had sacrificed it to the demon in exchange for more power. It was such an unthinkable breach that few would even suspect him of it.

Svendal knew that future sacrifices would someday prove inadequate. The Keeper would grow hungrier and hungrier; eventually, it would demand his own soul, as well.

He pursed his lips with determination. By then, I will have achieved my goal. I will be King Svendal, with more power than any king has ever known. When I have deciphered the runes on the chalice, I will know the secrets of the ancients. I will be able to control even Odowendus.

He was interrupted by a tap on his shoulder. He turned to see one of King Harben's magistrates, whom he considered one in a lineage of faceless civil servants.

"Yes?" he asked, impatiently. He noticed a peasant woman partially hidden behind the magistrate's robes, and he softened his tones. "What is it?"

"Master Svendal, this seems a case for your talents. The poor woman here has just borne a child, who is missing."

"Missing?" asked Svendal with raised eyebrows.

"Taken. Oh, please, my Lord," pleaded the woman, desperation winning over shyness. "He was stolen from me before he was an hour old. Have pity, Sir. Help me find him."

The magistrate murmured, "Forgive me, Master, you know how your reputation spreads among the poor."

Svendal held up his hand. "It's all right, Minister, I will see to it. Your baby is in good hands, dear woman."

"Oh, thank you, my Lord," gushed the peasant, and she fell to her knees, clutching onto Svendal's legs.

"Come now," said the magistrate, pulling her away. "Master Svendal is busy."

That I am, Svendal thought.

CHAPTER 10

Ragnar was in a foul mood. He would have given anything for a pitcher of Vitaqua. He was tired, cold, hungry and completely exasperated. The rude camp they had made in the shelter of a glade of pines was bitterly inadequate in the continuing snowfall.

He muttered, "It's been coming down for three days and nights, and it's colder than a virgin's lips."

He tried to conjure up the prospect of his own title and lands, of gorgeous maidens eager to wed him. It helped, but not as much as it had in the beginning.

He pulled out the bone. It still gleamed red on one end, but of what good was that? Every time he caught sight of his quarry, something drove him back. First, a tree had blocked his path. Then the party had been forced to avoid a pack of wolves. And always, the relentless snow fell.

He looked behind him. What was keeping the others?

It was all very well to have a talisman, but these men he had hired were useless. This was not turning out at all the way he had expected.

One of the soldiers came into view, a young, ruddy-faced peasant whose expression was one of utter resignation as he trudged through the knee-high drifts.

Ragnar started to vent his anger in his usual way, but instead he had a burst of practicality. I may not be a sorcerer, he thought, but I am no idiot.

"You, there. Bring me one of those traps you brought."

"Yes, my lord," called the soldier, pulling a large, iron wolf-trap from the saddlebag of his horse. He brought it over to Ragnar, and as ordered, placed it in the snow, primed it, and covered it again—somewhat unnecessarily, given the weather.

"Get another," ordered Ragnar.

The soldier hesitated.

"What is it now?" Ragnar asked.

"My lord, should we not mark them for our own

company? Else how will we avoid stepping into them?" The soldier's expression was compounded of equal parts mistrust and misery, which infuriated Ragnar.

"Of course, you fool. Make haste. Do you want us to freeze?"

From Magda Ranhubell's Journal ...

Thorn did not pester me again for the secrets of the chalice, and we maintained an uneasy truce while we continued to forge a trail through the snow forest.

The night after our food ran out, we stopped to rest, and Thorn was unable to find even a chokeberry bush to take the edge off our hunger. On impulse, I reached in to touch the chalice, and it was warm—and fragrant. I pulled it out, and set it on the ground, folding the bag around it to hide its lustrous runes from the magician's scrutiny. It was filled with rabbit stew.

We dipped our cups in it, too grateful to speak. Thorn was careful not to touch the chalice, but in the days to come it provided more than food to both of us.

The chalice gave warmth to our frozen hands and feet, in the lea of a pine or the overhang of a cliff while we waited out a flurry of the never-ending snow. Once an icicle fell into the chalice from a branch above, and the contents became a warming drink similar to Vitaqua.

Even so, the uphill climb and steady pelting of snow on my face eventually chafed my spirit to raw despair. This was the worst kind of snow. "Cutting White" we called it.

I was beginning to forget my own name, the chalice, or even the reason for my mission. The only thing left in my mind was that we must get over the Kloedrift Mountains before we were too tired to move, and were buried under layers of snow.

On the other side of the mountains would be Griffland. I yearned for a glimpse of the fabled hills and forests. Though I had never seen them, my imagination imbued them with a magical beauty.

When our path skirted the cliff above the fjords, I stopped, dizzy from looking at the sheer drop to the water below. This was nothing like the fjord near the Sanctuary of Ddiesana, which was barely an inlet in comparison.

The snow seemed to dance into oblivion, and the forest beyond curved gracefully around the crashing waves. I was struck silent by the beauty, and swayed on my feet. Just as I turned to call ahead to Thorn, I caught sight of a man whose form stood out dark against the snow-veiled trees.

I muffled a scream just as the man disappeared. My heart thudded in my breast, and I pulled off snow-encrusted mittens with my teeth, and reached into my coat to touch the chalice. Its warmth gave flexibility to my frozen fingers.

I wanted to cry, but some shred of pride enjoined me. I closed my eyes and prayed, instead. "Oh, Mother of Mothers, give me strength to go on."

Thorn came quietly to my side and waited, though he must have been hard pressed to restrain his impatience.

"You cried out. Did you see something?" he asked, when I had opened my eyes.

"A man. Perhaps the same one I saw before, but I cannot say. He is ahead of us, and not alone."

"What makes you say that?"

I shook my head. "I just know."

An owl hooted above us. Thorn looked up, shading his eyes from the snow. "Nanitma will guide us."

For a moment, our eyes met. Nanitma. The secret name. Our journey had given us little time for normal conversation since our argument. Now I saw a kindness in his look that made me blush. He, too, seemed overcome with emotion for he reached as if to touch me, then turned away.

With dogged steps, he was soon forging a trail through the dense, snow-drifted forest again, and having no choice, I followed.

The High Priestess Gostren sat in her room. As usual, she faced out the narrow, unglazed window, as she composed herself for her daily ritual. The snow fell relentlessly, softly, obscuring all but two hardy ravens pecking at the grain on her sill.

Resolutely putting aside her anxiety, Gostren breathed deeply, closed her eyes, and focused within herself. Into her meditation came a picture of the holy mountains of Kloedrift, the steep incline unraveling like a tree-embroidered tapestry before her. She held her breath.

At its foot, she could see the determined figure of Erik Ranhubell of Kenistar, with twenty of his men. Several leagues ahead of him was his son Ragnar, with half as many in his party, and finally, near the highest peak of the mountains were the young priestess and the magician.

Gostren's gift allowed her to see other things, too. Around Magda was a silvery light that winked in and out.

The chalice.

Above the travelers was a glowing, bluish light—at

first, she had feared it meant them harm, but now knew it was their ally—some sort of bird perhaps. It was obviously linked to the magician.

And last, on the old stone altar at the top of the mountains crouched a very different presence. A lumpy, noxious, dark green ember that pulsated like a boil. She could not discern its true shape. Gostren hugged herself and forced her mind to be calm. She sensed still another element in the tapestry—a different personality. This one started from the bottom of the mountains, ascending quickly.

Was it another bird? The way it moved—or flowed—a stream, perhaps. She rubbed her eyes. Her inner vision was not always easy to master.

She concentrated. The being had a light, was thus a living soul. And yet, it changed—first one shape, then another. She was reminded of dragons, said to have lived in other times.

The being moved slowly past the Earl and toward his son—and still Gostren could not identify it. Then she recognized him. She had worked with him once. She had been young and her gifts just beginning to reveal themselves, when she'd started as an apprentice healer in service to the Master. She had helped him save a child who otherwise would have died of the pox.

Svendal. Famous, wealthy, wise. Was he coming to help Magda? Gostren felt exultant. But as her inner eyes watched, joy faded. Her breathing stilled until it barely stirred her lungs, and her mind felt like congealed sap.

It was Svendal, yes, but not the Svendal she had known. As she watched, his figure flowed inexorably toward the two companions near the peak of the mountains. To Gostren's surprise, Svendal passed them, and his shadow moved toward the top where it finally resolved into solid form.

To some, it would appear to be a gnarled cedar like any other on the mountains. However, to the High Priestess, its sap was a rusted purple, with flecks of black and green, and brilliant spots of crimson and fuchsia. No ordinary tree, this.

Meanwhile, the figure that crouched on the altar pulsed stronger, a putrid green, the color of unholy life.

Gostren moaned and dug her fingers into her thighs as her hazel eyes snapped open.

"Oh, if I were more than an old healer, what I could do to that fiend." She balled her fists, roused by her own anger. She flexed her fingers and stood, a glow around her. Closing her eyes, she entreated, "Great Mother, in whose heart I live and whom I serve with every breath, help me send an ally to your daughter Magda."

Immediately into the tapestry of her inner mind there came a small white ember, like the flicker of a moth, as it swiftly flew for the top of the highest mountain. Just as swiftly, it was eaten up by the pustule on the altar, and Gostren fell back, almost tripping over the chair.

Gostren threw on her woolen shawl, and prepared to take her place at the morning meal. "This battle is not over yet," she muttered.

CHAPTER 11

For Ragnar, the day seemed endless. So far the traps had produced only a deer and two rabbits.

"No wonder Svendal sent us to do his work," he told a lieutenant. "The task is impossible."

Encouraged by this friendly mood, the soldier said, "My lord, the men are frozen to the bone. Perhaps we should turn back."

Ragnar blinked, trying to focus on the man's face through the snow flurries. "What is your name, soldier?"

"Dar, sir."

"Do you know these mountains, Dar?"

"Yes, sir. Like my hand. See that patch of trees ahead? They are too close for horses. And if we have not caught our quarry by then, we will be lamed by the cold."

Ragnar turned the problem over in his mind. His soul had burned with ambition for too long to give up Kenistar. The image of his father's estate loomed in his mind like the palace of the after-life. And more was promised if he succeeded in bringing back Magda and Thorn. His hand tightened over the bone in his pocket, and he looked up toward the highest peak of Kloedrift. He imagined himself buried with his men in an avalanche of snow. Was it worth it?

A wind of sense blew through Ragnar. He felt a pain lift from his soul like melting ice.

There was a legend about the Kloedrift Mountains, that they held a secret they would only reveal to those they favored. Ragnar felt he had been so favored, for he now knew that the secret was life. Life itself. Life was the real triumph, not lands and power. He considered for a moment that his sister was risking hers. And for what? A relic. If she does not listen to the mountains, he thought, it is not my fault.

"Lead us back, Dar. A wise goat does not butt his head against a stone."

The soldier grinned, and quickly relayed the news to the others, then said to Ragnar, "Master Svendal will be much displeased."

"Not as much as we will if we die on this mountain. We can hardly see a hand in front of us with this snow."

They had gone half a league when Ragnar heard a *crack* that made him clap his hands over his ears. He looked around. Had anyone else heard it? The members of his party were strung out now, completely hidden by the thickening swirls of snow, as they made their way slowly down the mountain.

Ragnar looked down. A sickly pool of red was spreading on the snow around him, and he wondered why he felt so little pain. The wolf trap had closed around his foot so neatly that it looked like a strange, enormous boot. His body toppled, and he screamed, but his voice was carried upward on the wind.

He raised his head and blinked, seeing only the intensifying blizzard.

With much difficulty, Ragnar managed to prop himself on his elbow, hoping against hope that a soldier might be wandering nearby, although his visibility was obscured. At this point, he would have even been happy to see Magda.

Big sister, he thought. They had been friends once. He remembered her giving him a ride on their father's horse when he was but a toddler. She had showed him how to catch treefrogs in the spring, and how to make a house of snow in the winter. Blood was dear. He'd forgotten it all, in the battle for his father's love.

"Father," he croaked.

Tears of rage and remorse seared his eyes, and immediately froze on his cheeks. This is my punishment for ambition, he thought.

Out of the snow came a dark form covered with black fur. Bear, he thought, his heart in his chest. The figure moved slowly through the snow.

What kind of bear leaves hibernation in a blizzard? It must be a mirage. Or worse, it must be Death himself come to stalk him in the guise of a bear. He had heard that Death did such things.

Ragnar groaned. The pool of blood on the snow was getting larger. He could hardly focus his eyes.

A voice called, "Ragnar ..."

Death—or the bear—had seen him then. What difference did it make? There was no escape.

Ragnar squinted through icy lashes at a frozen face, a grizzled, snow-flecked beard that reminded him of his father's. This was a bear trick. The Earl was not here. It was Death. Ragnar coughed, and he felt his lungs go numb with cold.

"He's lost much blood," said a voice.

"Go away," Ragnar rasped, then coughed again. Maybe if he conserved his strength, he could get his knife and throw it at the bear.

"If we do not find a healer soon, it will be too late, my Lord."

"Then, we will have to find one," bellowed a voice. It was exactly like the voice of his father.

"Leave me alone," croaked Ragnar. Another trick. Bears did not have healers.

He felt himself lifted into strong arms, and he screamed one time before he lost consciousness.

Buried under the blood-stained snow was the whitened bone he had carried.

In the guise of the gnarled cedar, Master Svendal used his far sight to watch the two struggling figures as they climbed. The sorcerer's form wavered in and out, first man, then tree, his arms becoming grasping limbs, his mouth a knothole.

"Soon, Master Odowendus," he rasped. "Victory is near enough to taste. The witchling had better treat my prize carefully." He flexed his fingers in the special gloves he'd crafted for this unique occasion.

The demon's feral eyes grew chilled as they measured the wizard as if for a coffin.

Svendal flinched away from the gaze, and said, "Her soul is yours—and his, as well, this Thorn whom I will pluck from my paw."

Odowendus said in his peculiar, silken voice, "You underestimate their power, mortal. Remember, if you fail, I'll have your soul instead."

"Fail?" sneered Svendal, and he began to recite an incantation which had the effect of making his tree form more solid.

The demon made no effort to disguise himself.

From Magda Ranhubell's Journal ...

As we climbed, my legs were getting more and tired. I would see the summit through a veil of falling snow, but it never seemed to get any nearer. Finally, just as I thought I would fall down from exhaustion, the top of the mountain came almost within reach.

I knew right away that there was something wrong. It was said the Kloedrift Mountains had been here since the time of the trolls, and that the mountains had a spirit of their own. But this was not the spirit of the mountains.

I had one hand in Thorn's, and one around the chalice whose warmth gave us strength and protection. The artifact did not speak to me as it had in the Sanctuary, but insinuated strange images directly into my mind. I wished for the twentieth time that I had begun the deeper training the High Priestess had suggested.

"Thorn," I said, "I feel the end is closer, now. We must hurry."

For days, I had held the clear vision of a stone altar before me—and I felt the chalice's desire for this resting place. I knew whatever else we found ahead, that I must place the relic in the center of the altar.

Thorn squeezed my hand. We were united now in our course, although the night before, we had quarreled. Overwhelmed by feelings of doubt and fear, I had given in to tears for the first time, while Thorn had tried to scold me out of my misery.

"Some priestess. Just look at yourself," he had scoffed.

"*Some magician,*" *I had countered, my voice rising with anger.* "*You haven't produced a single flame or scrap of food during our whole journey.*"

"*Fool,*" *Thorn had said.* "*Magic takes time—and discipline. Even the smallest effect means hours with the Keeper and memorizing hundreds of difficult words. Everything I do has a price.*" *Perhaps he was sorry for me then, because he had turned away, and moved out of earshot.*

Eventually, my tears had subsided, and I was sorry now, too, but had not been able to bring myself to speak of it.

Nanitma had been absent since the morning, and I wondered where the owl was. I squeezed Thorn's fingers back, but said nothing. He had nice fingers, strong and sensitive, and I felt a strange thrill at his nearness. I knew it was not appropriate for a priestess, but at the moment, I did not care.

Thorn seemed unaware of me, his eyes glued to the peak of the mountain looming just ahead. A large, misshapen tree presided over the summit, as if to prevent our passage. Thorn tensed.

I whispered, "*You feel it, too?*"

He glanced at me with his striking blue eyes. "*We*

must separate."

"No," I hissed.

He took my hand in both of his. "Be brave. When you see me move, take the fork to the right. Above all, do not go near that tree."

"What about you?"

He reached beneath his coat, and drew out an owl feather. "Whatever happens, do not be afraid, Magda Ranhubell."

I bit my lip to keep the tears inside. "Great Mother protect you, Thorn," I whispered, but I did not think he heard me, for he had already sprinted to the left.

I trudged up the path to the right, watching the tree from the corner of my eye. For a moment, I thought it moved, but I kept going.

When I had almost reached the top, I glanced to see where Thorn had gone, and paused in astonishment.

Standing on a prominent rock, holding the owl feather in his hands, Thorn's tall body reminded me of a strong bow from which an arrow might be launched. Before our eyes, his form dissolved into mist, leaving a flurry of snowflakes behind.

At a sound to my left, I saw the ugly tree dissolve, just as Thorn had done. I shivered, as a shadow covered me.

High overhead was a bird. Had Nanitma returned? Then, I saw it—that same, large bird that had appeared before. This time, I could see it clearly—a giant eagle with hooked talons and curved beak.

Its shadow cast a gloom over the whole area, and I gasped, feeling very small and alone. It was as if the shadow was a sponge that soaked up my will. I stumbled to my knees, clutching the chalice to my heart.

Another shape appeared in the sky, and I thought, "He has company. Soon there will be a flock of them. Oh, Great Mother, help me." But this second bird was no eagle. It was smaller, swifter, darker. This time, I was sure it was an owl. Was it Thorn's Keeper—or Thorn himself?

With darting feints, the two birds fought—first one and then the other—drawing blood with their hooked beaks. They rode the whipping wind like twigs in a mountain stream. Any minute, the owl might be killed. I was frantic. What could I do? I felt a twinge as if someone had pinched me.

The altar.

I looked, but saw only dark trees and a pock-marked

pile of moss or rotting leaves atop a construction of stones in the center of the summit.   As I gazed at it, I began to feel sick at my stomach.   Was that the altar?

CHAPTER 12

From Magda Ranhubell's Journal ...

The moss was breathing. For some reason, I felt completely helpless. I was like a leaf trapped in a block of ice, unable to take my attention from the mass of vegetation on the stone. With a choking fear, I knew—this enemy was much worse than the eagle.

My knees knocked, and fearful images from childhood surrounded me like ghosts. Was it a troll?

Troll or not, I knew that if I were to fulfill my task, I would have to get it to move from the altar.

The chalice burned within my fingers, and I felt even more afraid. The wind tore at my coat, and forced my hood back, exposing my fur hat to the full force of the elements. But a voice came into my mind. "Do not lose heart now—you are close."

The chalice had spoken to me at last. I forced myself to take a step nearer, and the warmth beneath my hands moved to my heart and belly, where it sat like a secret ally. I felt a spaciousness in my body, a power unlike anything I had ever known.

I took another step, and another, watching the mound carefully. The closer I came, the more it looked like a man, hunched over—a horrible, diseased man, perhaps. Or surely a troll. And still, this power in my body grew. I felt a tingling all along my scalp, and a warmth that defied the wintry cold.

Then the monster raised its head. Its face was covered with boils and scars, and its greenish skin glistened in the snow. Its expression was a grimace so evil it sucked the life out of everything around it.

Walking toward that face was worse than breasting the snow-laden wind. I reached into myself for calm. This morning, after a hasty First Light Meditation, I had felt Thorn's fingers linked with mine. "Together, we are stronger," he had said. I glanced into the sky, where the embattled owl and eagle still swooped and darted, jabbing with their claws and beaks.

I advanced another step toward the altar, still feeling as if I were wading through high snow. I could not let the troll see my fear.

Over the whistling of the wind, a scream came from the sky. I looked up and saw that the owl had torn a piece of the eagle's wing. But the eagle swerved downward, launching its talons into the owl's breast. The smaller bird was falling. I watched in horror as it disappeared beyond the crest of the cliff, and I imagined its beautiful body bloodying the rocks below, to be washed away by the crashing sea.

"Thorn," I cried. The wind grabbed my words like a ribbon as they whipped away from me. No one answered my call.

The eagle descended to a perch on a gnarled limb, one wing torn and bleeding. Its predatory eyes impaled me as it preened. I feared that it would strike at any moment.

The monster on the altar had not moved. It crouched patiently, unaffected by either snow or wind. The power of the chalice still ran in my veins, and I thought, Great Mother, what shall I do?

Be yourself, daughter, came the answer. Be myself? I was only a priestess, and not a fully trained one, at that. What did I know of trolls?

I searched my mind, but all I remembered were childhood tales to frighten me into obedience. Legend and hearsay would not help. But there were legends about the chalice, too, and its power to control evil. The wisdom of lullabies was whispered by mothers everywhere to their crying babes. What if it was all true?

Screwing up all my courage, I said, "Move away, troll, or I will burn you with the power of the sacred chalice. By the Goddess Herself, I command you."

The wind shrieked, and the monster gave a liquid laugh—a ripple of evil that echoed off the frozen trees. "You dare to insult me? I am Odowendus, Demon Lord of Underearth."

Demon. My teeth began to chatter, but the chalice burned in my hands and warmed my belly.

"Move away, then," I countered, my voice sounding weak compared to the demon's. I held my chin high. "Beware of that which I carry."

"That sorcerer's toy?" mocked the demon. "I am more interested in you, its bearer." As the monster said this, the eagle flew down from its perch, and began to circle me, a menacing shadow over the snow.

I sank to my knees, as the presence on the altar grew stronger. Icy snow swirled around me, biting into my skin. My face was raw. The fire in my belly was dimming, and my feet were beginning to feel the cold again.

I gripped the chalice. All it wanted was to be placed on the altar. It had a purpose beyond me. Why else had it spoken to me in the Chamber of the Goddess that day? Why else had I come this far?

The eagle screamed above me, and even with its one ragged wing, the bird swooped down, interposing itself between me and the altar. Instinctively, I raised my arms to hold the chalice between us. I watched the eagle's form dissolve, as it resumed the shape of the man I had seen earlier. He had the same black eyes and hair and beard, long, fur-lined cloak and rune-embroidered hat. Only now, there was blood on his right sleeve.

I quailed before him, shivering in the cold. He seemed unaffected by it, and bowed as if we were meeting in my father's Great Hall.

"Allow me to re-introduce myself, witchling. I am the Master Svendal. And you have something which should belong to me."

I looked down at the chalice. Its silvery surface glowed like molten, white fire in my hands. The reindeer seemed to prance and chase each other for some prize only they could fathom. What do I matter? I thought. I am only the messenger. The Chalice of the Silver Reindeer is the very soul of Montrovik, made by a power older than these mountains.

I glanced at Odowendus. The demon wants me, not the artifact, I reminded myself. If I must die, then that is my destiny. But first, I must deal with Svendal.

Rising to my feet, I said, "Great Svendal, you who once healed my father, what relation do you have to this fiend?"

The sorcerer laughed, as the demon had done, only Svendal's laugh was human, and somehow worse for its wickedness. "I do not fear the notorious Odowendus," said Svendal. "We are old friends." He flexed his fingers, and I noticed his gloves. They were made of a strange, green hide, resembling no animal I had ever seen.

"In fact, I'll make a bargain with you, witchling. Give me the chalice, and I'll protect you from the Lord of Underearth." He turned to the demon. "Are there not other ways of appeasing you, Lord Odowendus?"

"Careful, old friend," said the monster. Svendal's back become rigid. Fleetingly, I wished I had Thorn's knife. Despair washed over me. Thorn—did he now lie broken on the rocks? Oh, Mother, let it not be so.

The chalice burned in my hands, and I saw the demon's look of contempt when its glowing eyes lit upon the sorcerer. There was a chance, perhaps, that these two were *not united against me. After all, who could trust a demon—or a scoundrel like Svendal?*

"Hear me, Odowendus," I said. "I am a priestess of Ddiesana, gifted with the powers of the Mother. Whatever the sorcerer can offer you, it is nothing compared to me."

Svendal sneered at me. "You turnip. I gave you the chance to save yourself. Is this how you repay me?"

I gulped, ignoring the sorcerer's scowling face, and looked into the savage eyes of the demon. "Odowendus, I freely offer myself to you. Only move aside, and let me put the chalice down where you are sitting."

Before the demon could respond, Svendal lunged for the chalice. I gripped it, half-expecting him to recoil with singed hands, as Thorn had. However, I had not counted on the power of his gloves.

Their skin pulsed with green lightning, and he leered at me. "Let go, priestess, you are no match for me."

I gasped, feeling the sorcerer's foul breath on my face. My will felt like sleet. I forced myself to remember that I held in my hands a power that was older than legend—I must believe it was stronger than the sorcerer. As I wrestled with Svendal, I felt a tingling radiate to all parts of my body.

Svendal's brief expression of surprise at my

resistance was quickly replaced by determination. Little by little, his strength increased.

On the altar, the demon sat under its glistening coat of snow. Its hideous body expanded and contracted, with a patience born of long held desire.

"Let me have the chalice, witch," Svendal hissed. "You have no notion of its power. It has the force of both Light and Darkness. Without training, it will destroy you."

I gritted my teeth, as desperation rose in me. "The chalice uses its power to heal and protect, as you once did." I felt my belly fill with fire, my arms grow stronger. My legs felt rooted in the earth, as if I, too, were one of the gnarled cedars sculpted by the lashing wind and flying snow.

My scalp tingled, and my whole body felt as if it belonged to another. Svendal frowned and struggled even harder to wrest the chalice from me. The green lightning of his gloves crackled in the frozen air. "Let go, or I will hurt you. I can hurt you very badly," he warned.

"Go ahead. Whatever you do, I'm sure Odowendus can do worse." I could hardly form the words. I felt my voice blur, and could not tell whether Svendal had heard me. His eyes were narrow slits.

"Your last chance, witch," he grated. He started reciting words that bored into my soul. Slowly terror turned

my blood to ice with every word of his incantation.

I wanted to cry out, but could not. My hands and legs felt like packed snow, my eyelids were heavy. Amidst the fear and awe, I thought, It does not hurt at all.

Behind Svendal, the demon finally stirred.

CHAPTER 13

Under a woolen coat and fur-lined hood, Gostren felt the cold in her old bones, her back ached, and all her joints were pierced with needles of pain, but she continued to climb. On her back were provisions, herbs, a wool blanket, and little else. Her spirit guides had told her she would not need them if she failed.

She remembered the first vision she had ever had. A child of six, she had been on her father's lap at a circus. The traveling entertainers had done cartwheels and leapt into the air, while she laughed delightedly.

The main event was a pair of dancing reindeer. They were pure white, with colored bridles. They moved in unison, their dainty hooves sketching lovely patterns in the snow.

When they were almost finished, Gostren had seen a monster enter the ring. He'd mounted a reindeer, and his ugly face had leered in the firelight. He was bright green, covered with sores, and his hideous grin had mocked her. The little girl had screamed and screamed. No one had ever understood what had so terrified her.

Gostren remembered this now. And as she remembered, she thought of the evil presence she had envisioned that morning.

She was interrupted by the sound of men and horses. Erik Ranhubell? But he should be far ahead by now.

Worried, she peered ahead. As the voices came closer, she saw a thick-set figure she recognized, but for all his strength, she could see that sorrow slowed his movements.

"Earl," she called. "Over here."

Gostren saw him stop and turn her way. When Erik recognized the High Priestess, he bounded through the snow like a young man, yelling excitedly. "My prayers are answered. A healer."

Gostren sighed. It was the son, then. She had already seen the shape of death, felt the atmosphere of doom hovering over the party. With a brittle smile, she let Erik lead her through the frozen trees toward the robe-wrapped figure on the horse.

The priestess lowered her pack, and felt inside the robe for Ragnar's pulse. It was a few moments before she could find it. She put her cheek down to his mouth, and felt the icy breath of disease.

Gostren said to the men, "Lower him, but first pile all the blankets you have into a bed. And be ever so careful— he dwells now in the world between ours and the land of the Mother." She pressed her fingers into Erik's arm. "You must breathe for him, let your heart beat for his, your will be his will. Together, we will bring him back."

When Ragnar had been laid upon the blankets, Gostren pulled a bag of herbs from her pack, and unpeeled her snow-covered gloves. With trembling fingers, she drew out a twig upon which two wizened leaves clung. She crushed the leaves with her thumb and forefinger, and then moistened the powder with spittle, making a paste. With this, she painted Ragnar's lips.

Putting one hand over his heart, Gostren prayed, as gradually, Ragnar licked the paste from bluish lips, and sighed.

Erik cried, "He moved. He is alive."

"Quiet," said Gostren. "He is not with us yet." Carefully, she stroked the air around his leg with her wrinkled hands, and prayed again. "Oh, Great Mother, if this father's love be true, let him bind this soul to the earth for awhile yet. Stay your desire to bring him home, and help this son of Montrovik to walk your forests and mountains once again."

Whatever their misgivings, neither Erik nor his men said a word. The wind had died, and the snow, which had fallen mercilessly for days, subsided.

Ragnar blinked. Immediately, Gostren grabbed two handfuls of snow with her bare hands, and pressed them into the gash that had nearly separated Ragnar's leg.

"Stop," Erik cried. Grabbing a blanket, he threw it over Ragnar's bloodied leg, then covered it with his own body, stretching out his hide-covered hands and arms. "Don't touch him," he commanded the healer.

Gostren sat back on her heels, and took a deep breath. "Get up, Earl," she said.

The Earl raised his chin, and looked at his son, whose pale blue eyes had stopped their restless darting, and were now fixed on his. In that look a bond formed between them that transcended all the cruel times, the bitter words and actions that had brought them so much pain.

"Father," said Ragnar. "You're not a bear."

"No? Just wait until I get you home," Erik scolded, but there were tears in his eyes.

Gostren said, "He is not going home."

"What?" said Erik.

"Look," said Gostren, and pointed to Ragnar's blanket-covered legs.

Trembling, Erik lifted the blanket, and gasped. The leg was whole, untouched, as if it had never been pierced by iron or even snow.

"Forgive me, Your Eminence. You are a performer of wonders," he breathed. "What payment can I give you?"

"Nothing." Gostren shook her head. "It was you who healed him."

"But—" stammered Erik. "There must be a price. When Master Svendal cured me of the fever, I paid him one hundred sovereigns."

Gostren felt chilled. "When magic is used to heal, there is always a price. But in true healing, the sufferer's pain is his payment."

She looked upwards, toward the towering cliffs at the peak of the mountains. "There is another who needs my aid, and I cannot get there without help."

"I will gladly help you," said Erik, "for that is a price I understand. Son, you need to go home. You have been on the mountain several days and are nearly frozen."

"No, Father," said Ragnar. "I must lead you. Otherwise, how will you find the traps?" He stood up, eagerly, testing his legs as if he were a newborn colt. There was no pain. He was not even cold.

"Ivar, get Lord Ragnar a new pair of boots from the pack horse," ordered Erik. "Lars, stow away these blankets." He turned to Gostren. "Your Eminence, take my horse."

In a few moments, Gostren was mounted, the feeling of elation soon displaced by the foreboding that had brought her here. Her sense of doom was still strong, and cold anger weighted her heart, remembering the green monstrosity on the circus horse, grinning with its evil secret.

From Magda Ranhubell's Journal ...

I could not think. The sorcerer's hands grasped mine upon the chalice, and though I writhed to get free, his strange gloves crackled with green fire that made me a prisoner.

Meanwhile, the demon had shuffled to the very edge of the altar. It must have been difficult for it to move, because it only inched slowly along, and its body wavered in form as if it took concentration to make it solid.

Svendal, however, was as strong and agile as a young man. From gritted teeth, he said, "You and the chalice are mine, now, Magda. Your beauty, your youth, your passion, combined with the fire of the artifact, will make me the most powerful king in history."

Odowendus spoke in its hideous tenor, "That was not our bargain, sorcerer. What game do you play?"

"No game," said Svendal. "Once I have extracted the power from the artifact, I will release the witchling into your hands, Keeper."

"Not acceptable," said Odowendus. "I want her now or I will have you." The atrocity shuffled over the lip of the altar, leaving a sizzling trail of ooze that melted the snow before it evaporated.

With all my strength, I spoke at last, beseeching the Goddess and whatever ancient power resided in the chalice. "May the Great Mother and all the Powers of Earth free me from this evil."

The sorcerer blinked, as if he had not expected a mere girl to attempt to counter him. In that instant of his hesitation, I managed to wrench from Svendal's grasp, and throw myself upon the altar, the chalice hugged to my heart.

The demon reached for me, catching my sleeve as I rushed past. A putrid scent filled my nostrils and burning oil sizzled through the cloth and onto my skin. I screamed as I landed on sharp stones, feeling the scrape tear through my robe and leggings. A blazing light erupted from the altar, singeing my hands and knees. It was a blinding white— even brighter than the sun glinting off new snow.

I gritted my teeth, and inched closer to the center of the altar. I groaned with the agony of my burning hands, and tear-scalded eyes. Feeling as if my skin were welded to the chalice, I placed the holy object into the center of the light—the circular hollow in the middle of the stone.

The demon screamed, a high pitched sound that leached all sense from my mind. I turned to see the monster grab for Svendal, who stood as still as a block of ice. Just as the hideous hands touched the sorcerer, Odowendus seemed to melt. Beneath him, the ground opened up, and a hole in the earth itself began to suck the Lord of Underearth into the realm from which he came.

I clung to the altar, while a stream of shadows

emanated from Master Svendal, merging with the river of slime that had been the demon's form. Unable to help myself, I watched in frightened fascination as these essences seeped into the hole, which closed behind them with a slap that echoed against the rocks, leaving Svendal standing alone.

CHAPTER 14

From Magda Ranhubell's Journal ...

Feeling triumphant, I was unable to think clearly. All I knew was that I had succeeded in bringing the chalice to its destination. I raised my eyes to the pale, distant sun, and yelled, "Praise to the Mother of all Mothers."

My voice echoed down the mountain like a song. Exhaustion filling my lungs, I climbed down from the altar. My hands no longer burned, and they were unmarked. I looked at Svendal. His face was a study in rage, and I felt something in me burst.

What did my life matter now? I had done my part. A laugh escaped me. "Your Keeper has deserted you, Master Svendal. Give thanks that the Goddess has allowed both of us to live."

With an unearthly howl, the sorcerer turned from me

and lunged for the chalice. Horrified, I realized I would never be able to intercept him. I cried out as his gloved hands wrapped around the chalice. He screamed with agony, and I soon saw the reason. Now that the chalice was in its rightful place, the magic in his gloves was absorbed by the artifact. He was unable to take his hands away from it.

Turning his head with effort, he looked at me and said, "You know my power. If I cannot have the chalice, then I will destroy it. I have not come this far for nothing."

"No," I cried, and climbed back onto the altar, my feet slipping in the snow. I leapt onto Svendal's back, trying with all my might to pry him from the chalice. He threw me off like an ant, and I landed painfully on the altar stones.

Kneeling on all fours, I called on the Goddess for a last ounce of strength. In that instant, something extraordinary took place. The tingling in my scalp intensified. My hands and feet itched, and a billowing force rippled in my belly where the fire of the chalice had once been.

My hands were hooves. My skin was covered with silvery white fur. Upon my head were velvety antlers.

I pranced on the altar, feeling the wet flakes on my nose, the wind in my fur. Below me, Master Svendal was a dark blob in the middle of the blazing light from the chalice.

He howled with pain again as his gloves turned to ashes. I watched them sprinkle like powdered snow onto the stones, and his hands finally came unglued from the chalice by a supernatural force beyond his control. His palms were seared with silver runes that matched the ones on the chalice.

Still not seeing me, he slid to the ground, and sank to his knees, searching for the hole that had swallowed his ally.

"Forgive me, Keeper, I have failed you." He pounded the earth with his fists while the wind lifted his black hair so that it appeared he had wings.

A voice came out of my mouth, though I had no control over it: "I was your first Keeper, remember? Before the stag, before the bear, before the abominations you learned to conjure. You had power and skill—the ability to heal and help, transform and teach. And you abused them."

At last, Svendal looked up, shading his eyes against the vision, and something in the mage's face crumbled. A long imprisoned ray of truth shone from his eyes, and his teeth chattered with fear.

"Forgive me," Svendal cried. "I will make amends."

"That you shall, but not as a sorcerer, old man." The

mountain was suddenly wreathed in mist, and I quivered at the knowledge of the ancient powers that lived here. Something momentous was happening, but I could see only a cloud of white. Had I stepped into a realm of magic where I would be forever exiled from my family, the Sanctuary—and Thorn?

As mysteriously as it had come, I felt my reindeer form dissolve. I touched my chest with my mittened hand, felt my face, and looked down at my familiar garments. My braids were all in disarray, and I combed the last of them out with my fingers, letting my red hair hang free around me. Had I imagined it all?

The wind had died. When had it stopped snowing?

Master Svendal sat on the icy ground—at least, I knew it was him by his clothing, for his beard and hair had become white, and his face bore the lines of age once hidden by his sorcery. He sat in his fine cloak and boots, staring into the distant horizon, where an aura of snow clouds gathered around a hazy needle of sun.

I looked toward the altar, and the chalice glowed with the inner fire that was even stronger now. As before, it spoke to me in my mind, with a voice like silver. "You have done well, Magda, but you must follow your own destiny now. Our time together is finished."

I remembered my first encounter with the chalice in the Sanctuary, and all that had occurred since.

I bit my lip. Follow my own destiny? Since my destiny had been wedded to that of the chalice, I had lost my way. What was next?

I looked out over the cliffs where the forests of Griffland massed like clumps of moss. I could not see the wave-tumbled rocks that glistened by the shore. I turned toward Montrovik, and started down the path, calling, "Thorn ... Thorn?"

I had not gone ten steps when I was greeted by the hoot of an owl. I looked up at the brown and white bird in the tree above me. It had no dark spot on its breast.

"Nanitma?" I whispered.

The owl flew down, and landed on the snow at my feet. Its eyes were dark blue, like the fjords at midnight.

"Thorn," I cried. I knelt to touch him, and the owl dissolved, replaced by a tall, dark-haired man in a coat lined with white fur, with rune-embroidered sleeves. He pulled me up and gathered me into his arms.

"Magda," he whispered, stroking my hair. He tensed, squeezing my arms. "Are you all right?"

I pulled up my sleeve and saw that the burn to my arm had left a streak of white, but I felt no pain.

Thorn said, "I am sorry I failed you."

I looked up at him. "You risked your life." I looked him over with concern. "Where is your wound?"

He gave a wry smile, his eyes misty. "I lay half dead on the rocks, sure that I was on my way to meet the Goddess. I dreamed a silver-furred reindeer came to me and licked my wounds. When I awoke, I was completely healed." Thorn squeezed my arms. "As an owl, I flew to the top of the mountain where I saw a shining reindeer."

I caught my breath, about to tell him—

"I knew that it was you."

I smiled. "The whole thing seems like a dream. Was it all that you hoped—being another creature?"

He nodded. "Now you know why I sought to ride the power."

"Perhaps I, too, have a Keeper now," I said, shyly. Could a priestess also be a magician?

Thorn gazed at me with serious eyes. "Would you consider coming to court, or are you still bound to the Sanctuary?"

"I am bound—to no one," I said, wondering how much of my thoughts he had guessed. "What would I do at court?"

"Help me teach the others how to honor their Keepers and the Goddess, as well. How to keep the balance in a world of ice and sun. Now that the chalice is restored to its true home, the powers of darkness are banished forever. We have the rest of our lives to learn the secrets of good."

I liked his words. I searched his eyes for more. "I am not sure I want to know any secrets."

"No?" he said, and pulled me close to him. Trembling, I watched as he leaned down, then I closed my eyes as his mouth met mine. I felt my body become as insubstantial as a shape-shifter—a different kind of shape-shifter. Perhaps he was right. Some secrets might be worth exploring.

"Are you suggesting we marry?" I asked when I could breathe. I didn't even know Thorn's full name, only that he had spoken of being raised in a village, not an estate like Kenistar. I could imagine what my father would say.

Thorn smiled. "If you'd have me, though I know better than anyone what a terrible temper you've got, even for a woman."

We laughed. I held his hands, and looked away, back toward the peak of the mountains, where I had left

Svendal staring witlessly at the sky. Was I still a priestess—or not? What was my destiny?

I was distracted by the sound of a party of men approaching, and I glanced at Thorn. "I—"

"We can talk later," he shook his head, settling my blanket around my shoulders. "Your lips are blue. Let's go."

When I turned around, the first person I saw was my brother.

CHAPTER 15

Ragnar jumped down from his horse. Without a trace of injury, he bounded over the snow toward Magda, and when he reached her, glanced gratefully at Thorn, then clasped his sister in his arms.

"Thank the Goddess, you're safe," he cried.

"Ragnar?" Magda was astonished. She hugged him back, feeling cold, unable to absorb any more shocks.

Thorn called to one of Erik's men, "Find her a blanket before she freezes."

Ragnar said, "Thank you for her safety, sir. I expect your name is Thorn, but do not ask me how I know."

Thorn said, "I care not, only that you get us off this mountain. I will be happy if I never set foot upon it again."

Magda received the saddle blanket from the man,

and settled it around her, feeling warm and displaced, as if she were someone new, someone she had always wanted to be but never imagined she could be.

Erik joined them, his eyes sparkling at the sight of his disheveled daughter. He thought he had never seen anyone more beautiful, and he enfolded Magda in his arms. "Can you ever forgive me?" he whispered, gruffly.

"Ssh," said Magda. "Ssh, now."

When he had wiped the moisture from his eyes, complaining of the mist in the air, the Earl fancied he saw a certain friendliness between his daughter and the tall young man. "Your name, lad? And where is your family?"

"I am Thorn Litvar, from Traenna, a village holding. My father is Chief Elder—Gunter Litvar. We have three herds of reindeer and my brother Për already has a wife. I intend to wed your daughter, Lord Ranhubell, with or without your consent."

"Well, well," said Erik, frowning. "You have mettle, if not manners. Let us get safely home, before we talk of marriage." He glanced to see Magda's reaction, but she had gone to help Gostren dismount.

"High Priestess, what are you doing here?" said Magda, taking the older woman's hands.

"The usual reason, Daughter," said Gostren. "I was called." She looked at Magda sternly. "As were you, I take it. You should have told me."

Magda blushed, then lifted her chin.

Gostren put her arm around her. "The Great Mother was with you, Daughter. I am glad you are well." She pulled Magda aside. "What is left on that mountain?"

Magda looked up toward the peak. "The chalice resides where it belongs, upon the holy altar. The demon has been banished." She looked at Gostren. "The evil sorcerer Svendal sits staring at the sky as if it holds his fate."

Gostren sighed. "It does. I must go to him."

"Leave him, Your Eminence," Magda protested. "He would have killed us all to have the power of the chalice."

Gostren snorted. "I always knew you were a warrior, not a priestess. You were raised on horseback, and even six winters in the company of women did nothing to soften your edges, Magda. Have pity, child. A power like Svendal is not tossed away like a broken pot." She patted Magda's cheek, and proceeded up the path toward the peak.

"You are not going alone, Your Eminence," said Magda.

"But I am. Be sure no one follows," Gostren ordered.

Beyond the trees, Gostren saw a hunched figure, old and wrinkled. The man was muttering to himself, and she could not make out the words. When she got closer, she was distracted by a silvery light. She stopped to gaze at the Chalice of the Silver Reindeer as it gleamed in the sunlight.

"Oh, Mother of Mothers, it is beautiful," she whispered.

She approached the white-haired old man, and marveled at the change that had come over him. She would not have recognized him. He had the same long nose, but his face and hands were a mass of spidery lines, and he peered up at her with black eyes that had lost their fire.

"Svendal?" she said, holding out her hand.

With a baleful look at the altar, the old man rose to his feet, grunting and groaning. His back was bent with age, and he leaned on the High Priestess' arm. Gostren marked the uncertainty in his movements.

"You were a powerful sorcerer once—a wise teacher," said Gostren. "I am sorry for what has happened to you."

"Sorry—for me?" he asked, with a sparkle of the old spirit. "I'll—I'll ..." He knew there was something he wanted to do, but could not remember how to do it. He picked up his hat from the snow, and looked at the runes embroidered in it. He knew they meant something, but for the life of him, he knew not what.

There were runes burnt into his hands, too. He marveled at them, deeply frustrated that he could not understand them at all.

"Where are you taking me? What is to become of me?" he whined, looking this way and that.

Gostren ignored him. Raising her hands, she said, "I dedicate this holy place to the Great Mother, and from this moment forward, no evil can set foot upon it." The ground beneath her feet rumbled in answer, and the chalice winked at her with a glancing ray of eldritch light.

Svendal trembled and shrank nearer to the High Priestess. "Take me home," he pleaded, in a voice that contained but a ghostly shred of the old authority.

Thorn and Magda watched until Gostren came into view, supporting Svendal, who was obviously having a hard time of it.

"It is a mystery why the Mother permitted him to live," said Magda.

"He paid his Keeper with his soul," said Thorn.

Magda looked at the once-powerful sorcerer. He walked like a lost child. It was hard to imagine him taunting a demon. "Now that the evil has been banished, he is empty. Perhaps the High Priestess will give him new purpose. That is her talent."

When they came closer, the old man shrank at the sight of Thorn.

Even at a distance, Thorn could see the silver tinged runes on the shriveled hands. He looked down. The marks where Thorn's hands had first touched the chalice had faded completely.

"Those runes are the ones on the chalice," he whispered to Magda.

"Yes, but no one can read them—even the oldest sage of our Sanctuary. It is said they were carved by the Goddess herself in an ancient script older than time."

His eyes narrowed. "Is that so?" He walked toward Svendal, and Magda followed, frowning.

The old man acted as if he did not know the young magician, although it was plain to see he recognized him only too well.

He and Thorn stared at each other, and Thorn nodded. "Hello, Master."

Svendal trembled, clutching onto Gostren.

"Your Eminence, may I examine his hands?" asked Thorn.

Gostren raised an eyebrow. "Do you think you can read them?"

He shrugged. "I can try."

"We shall both try," said Magda, feeling bold. She glanced at the High Priestess Gostren, but the old woman's face was as smooth as a lake.

Magda took one hand, Thorn the other. Svendal quivered, angry and afraid.

Thorn said, "It looks like the character for *life*—or is it *moon*?"

Magda closed her eyes, feeling the runes with the pad of her thumb. The image of a beautiful lady appeared, clothed in pale blue. Her smile made Magda feel more protected than she had ever felt, as if she had come home. Her knees trembled.

"It is a message from the Goddess," she said, wonderingly. "It means, 'Never fear.'"

You see?" said Thorn, taking both her hands. His eyes were earnest. "You have much to teach. Come to court with me, and we will learn from each other."

Magda's mouth opened, and she groped for words. "I am still a novice. I never had the deep training." She glanced at Gostren.

The High Priestess smiled. "You have the sight, child," she said.

Thorn laughed. "It is a long way to the bottom of these mountains. I'll convince you yet, my girl." He took Magda's arm. "Thank you, Your Eminence."

When they neared the horses, a man stepped forward, leading a gray mare. It was Ingemar, one of Erik's men.

"Help the lady, would you?" said Thorn, indicating Magda.

"Her?" said Ingemar.

Magda leapt onto the mare's back, then looked down at Thorn.

"Help the man, Ingemar," she laughed. Thorn hoisted himself up behind Magda, and together they rode with the others toward the Great Keep of Montrovik, King Harben's stronghold.

CHAPTER 16

It took only three days to return home, now that the snowfall had stopped. Erik had promised provisions and beds enough for all when they reached the Keep, and there was laughter and relief in the faces reflected in the campfires each night on the journey.

Even Gostren agreed she would spend one night before leaving for Ddiesana. It was uncertain whether Magda would accompany her. The High Priestess kept silent on the subject, and Magda followed her example.

To those of the camp, Magda dwelt in a world apart, and they whispered about her. Some tried to touch her as she passed. She had a smile for all who spoke to her, but stayed close to her family and Thorn.

During the journey, Thorn admired the way Magda deftly turned the horse this way and that among the gnarled cedars and tall pines, as if she were one with the animal. He had insisted on riding behind her, an easy request to satisfy since they were short of horses. He loved the smell of wood smoke in her bright hair and the look of her small, square shoulders.

On their way, they talked of many things, shared confidences they had not had time for during their treacherous ascent. On the last day of their journey, they were riding apart from the others. The sun was just setting and the spires of Kenistar appeared before them. At the sight, he resolved to kiss her.

"Slow down, Magda," he coaxed, clasping her around the waist. She responded by nudging the gray mare into a gallop that took them over a stream, and through another hill and wooded area before rejoining their party. Now that the mountains were behind them, the horse was frisky in spite of fatigue, glad to be headed home.

Thorn said, "Just what I would expect from a wild thing like you. Marry me, and you can ride as fast as you wish."

Magda tossed her head, and the wisps of ermine fluttered around her face. "Wild, am I? It's you that carries a knife, remember?" She dug her heels into the horse's flanks. The mare would be overheated, but Magda did not care.

Erik Ranhubell stroked his beard, which he had oiled and combed into a neat gray fork, as befitted a man of his station. He smoothed a crimson, velvet tunic over his ample belly.

He had not had time for a private word with his daughter since they had left the mountains. The night of their arrival at Kenistar, the King had arrived with venison and servants, and hosted a banquet in honor of the heroes. Despite the ragged appearance of the weary travelers, it had been a formal affair, offering no opportunity for intimate conversation. The Great Horn was passed around again and again, with many a speech and rousing cheer.

Erik had been gratified to see that King Harben was himself again. He also noted that Ragnar was showing a new maturity and had not touched a drop of Vitaqua.

Erik nodded to himself, "He will not waste another winter."

He closed the door to his suite of chambers, and traversed the long passageway leading to the women's quarters. Implements of warfare along the walls gave way to delicate tapestries depicting the shearing of lambs in spring and the bathing of newborn babies in the streams of Kloedrift in summer.

He smiled. It would be good to have a female presence in the house again. That is, if he were successful. "The girl must be made to see sense," he muttered, making an unconscious fist. One of the tapestries caught his eye.

In it a young girl rode a horse. She was very like Magda. Erik ran his rough fingers over the satin. She was a wild thing, Magda. Like her mother. Sense was not in her—not his sort of sense, at least.

He reflected that they had quarreled many times over such things, and if he were to get anywhere with her, he should perhaps hear her views first. With an ironic smile, he saluted the figure in the cloth. "Thank you, Milady," he said, then cleared his throat, looking around to be sure he had not been noticed.

When he reached Magda's quarters, he knocked, and said, "Magda?"

"Father! Come in," she said.

Erik hardly recognized her. Her long, bright hair was neatly braided with a red ribbon. She wore a dark green dress under a brushed woolen tunic of bright blue, held by two silver brooches shaped like reindeer heads with amber beads strung between. In her ears were the delicate silver snowflake pendants King Harben had given her. They each sparkled with a crystal gem in the center. At the banquet, the monarch had offered her a whole bag of jewels from his coffers, but this was all she would accept.

"Bless your fingers and toes," said the Earl.

"And yours," she said. They made their way toward the hearth, and Magda gave Erik the bigger chair.

He settled into it gratefully, stretching his large hands toward the fire, and propping his feet upon the grate.

When he was warm, Erik sat back, looking at his daughter with approval. "The last time I saw you, you barely came up to my chin. Now look at you."

She raised her eyebrows. "It's the plain food and hard work I did at the Sanctuary." She looked down for a moment. "Father, I never wanted to hurt you. When I ran away—"

"I blame myself, not you, Mag," he said, noticing that her eyes got misty at the use of the pet name. "They must have treated you well, there," he said gruffly.

"The very best, Father," said Magda, staring at the fire.

Erik's heart sank. He had not the will to ask her what he had come for. Suddenly he felt old.

With uncanny timing, Magda said, "I'm not sure I

want to return to Ddiesana."

Erik noticed the care she had taken with her clothes, her braided, beribboned hair, the precious earrings, the dress and tunic. "I see you have put aside your drab robes," he said.

"For now." Magda looked up. "I need to think."

Erik blurted, "You belong at Kenistar. It is your home. Not as regent—not if you don't wish it. Come and go as you will."

Magda would not look at him, and there was confusion on her face. She seemed full of emotion, maybe on the brink of tears.

Erik thought he would never understand women. "Did I say something amiss?" he asked.

She shook her head. "My memories of Kenistar are the happiest of all. Riding and falconry, waking up to the sound of your yapping dogs and the smell of spiced apples and winterberry muffins." She gazed at the fire. "It's just— I am not sure who I am. In my brief lifespan, I have been an heiress, a priestess, and even an outlaw. I need time."

Erik was silent while a log crackled. "Why did you disobey the laws of Montrovik? What made you take the chalice?"

Magda pulled her feet up into the chair, reminding Erik of the child she had been. She looked intently into his face. "I know you never speak of her, but I must. I do not remember my mother. I knew nothing of a woman's feelings, of sensitivity or trusting my inner voice, my visions."

Erik cleared his throat, focusing on a torn spot in the hide of his boot.

"Perhaps that is why the Goddess led me to the Sanctuary. There I learned the ways of women. I began to hope that I had a small gift, maybe a calling. When the chalice spoke to me, I could not believe it. Why had it chosen me and not an older, more experienced priestess? I was afraid—afraid of what it charged me with—of the mountains, the cold, the dishonor I would bring on myself and the Sanctuary."

"Then, why?" repeated Erik.

"Because of you, Father."

"Me? What nonsense." He frowned.

She touched his arm. "It was you who taught me to have the courage of a man. To follow what I believed in, no matter what, no matter who was against me. None of the other priestesses had the Ranhubell courage, no matter how they might try."

Erik's heart felt doubled in size. He slapped his knee. "I always said you were the son I should have had, Mag."

"No, Father. I was the daughter," she said in a soft voice. "And you must let me go to find my destiny—just as you would if I were your son. Do you understand?"

Erik frowned. He was not a man of imagination, but he understood blood. No Ranhubell liked to be told what to do. "I will do my best," he said.

Magda beamed, "Thank you."

Erik cleared his throat. "What of this man, Thorn? He seems a wild sort."

"Him?" said Magda, looking away. "He was kind to me—and brave. We are good friends, bonded by the dangers we have survived together."

"No more?" asked Erik, narrowing his eyes.

"I admire him, but he is a peasant, Father," she said, with a sidelong glance at Erik, and a deep sigh. There were two red spots on her cheeks.

Well, well, he thought. My daughter is in love, or I don't know a spoon from a sword.

"Hmm," Erik said, stroking his beard. "So, you think he is not good enough for you?"

"Oh, no. It's … he is fine, but are there not laws I must follow? About marriage, I mean. Of course, I may never marry. Or I may never marry him." She seemed to have a lump in her throat.

"It's good to hear you speak of laws, Daughter," said Erik. "Marry whom you will. By the Goddess, do you think I've learned nothing these past winters?" He chuckled. "It's good to think of you settling down."

Magda shrugged and picked off a nonexistent piece of lint from her tunic. Erik was struck by her resemblance to Ragnar. *She's hardly more than a boy, at that,* he decided. *It will be interesting to watch her turn into a woman.*

He rose. "Well, I must go and see to provisions for the King's journey home. You will let me know what you decide?" He held her shoulders. "You have my blessing, whatever it is."

"Thank you, Father," she said, and her eyes were less troubled than before.

He kissed her cheek, and made his way to the Great Hall to find the steward.

CHAPTER 17

From Magda Ranhubell's Journal ...

I was glad to have bathed at last, and hoped to never again see the clothes I had worn on the Kloedrift Mountains. Here, there had been no simple robes befitting a priestess. This was Kenistar, where fine costumes were plenty.

I smoothed the long, green dress over my hips, and touched the soft wool of the bright blue over-tunic. I had taken a look at myself in the burnished glass over the mantle, and my earrings reminded me of the glimmer of the chalice, which was why I had chosen them. Whenever I wore them, I wanted to remember the words of the Goddess: Never fear.

My sense of duty as a priestess still tugged at my heart. The advice of the chalice echoed in my mind: follow your own destiny now.

My father's visit had left me feeling nervous. I was not ready to see Thorn.

I sat in the large chair my father had vacated. It was good to have a civilized fire in a real hearth. I thought of my sisters at the Sanctuary, living in rooms barely large enough for a bed and table.

A knock sounded on the door, and I jumped. Then I recognized Gostren's distinctive triple tap, and I hurried to let her in, curtseying, then giving her a hug, not knowing what was seemly.

She laughed. "Sister Magda, don't you look lovely."

"Thank you, Your Eminence. It has been a long time since I have had such nice things to wear. Oh, I didn't mean—"

"I understand. The life of a priestess is one of attention to the details within, and the simpler we can make our outer lives, the better. Still, there is nothing wrong with beauty." Gostren settled herself in a cushioned chair by the fire.

"And how is your patient, Master Svendal?" I asked.

She folded her hands into the sleeves of her gray, woolen robe. "He is coming along. Perhaps we can teach him to tend to the plants in the conservatory at Ddiesana.

He seems willing to learn, though he is old and slow." She laughed. "The sisters will quite love him, I think."

"Great Mother," I exclaimed. "It is hard to believe."

Gostren nodded. "Change is always difficult at first, which brings me to the reason for my visit."

I held my breath. I had received nothing but praise for my actions by my father and brother, and even the King and his ministers. The notice branding me an outlaw had been burned. Still, the High Priestess had said nothing of my rash actions since that day on the mountain. Was I finally going to receive my punishment for desecrating my vows of obedience as a priestess?

"My Daughter," said Gostren, "do you wish to be released from your commitment to the Sanctuary?"

I swallowed and looked down at my hands to avoid those sharp hazel eyes. "What makes you think—?"

"Magda, I have a certain intuition, remember? It is part of my job. It is not the ribbon in your braids that tells me you have changed. It is what lies in here." She tapped her chest. "I know you have been asked to marry Thorn Litvar of Traenna."

"Yes, Your Eminence," I said.

"And what of your inheritance?"

It was not what I had expected her to say, and I stumbled over my words. "My father will give it to Ragnar. I—I never wanted it, anyway."

"Well, then," said Gostren. "That leaves you two options, at least. And remember, there are others."

I nodded.

"I am eager to know what you yourself believe is your course now. Are you still a priestess of Ddiesana?"

Gostren's eyes had become as hard as acorns. I shrank from her searching gaze. What did she want of me? "I—I do not think so," I said. It had not been what I had wanted to say, but as soon as it was out, I knew it was true.

She sighed. "Very well, then. I had once thought ... but that was before the Goddess chose you for another task."

Instinctively, we both looked toward the mountains.

"Do you love him?" asked Gostren.

"Yes," I said.

"Then, your heart has spoken."

I looked down.

"What's wrong, child?" asked Gostren.

I blurted. "Your Eminence, I am like the chalice. I want to have my own place. I do love him, but—" I caught my breath. "I am afraid to lose my wildness. For all my life, it was all I had." I put my palms to my burning cheeks.

Gostren laughed. "I think that is the least of your worries. He is no sled dog. Why do you think he will make you into one?"

I shook my head. "I know nothing of the ways of marriage."

Gostren leaned forward, and took my hand. "Magda, all ways are the ways of the Goddess. Follow your heart." She rose, and I followed her to the door.

"One more thing," Gostren said, her hazel eyes pinning me with their fire. "If it had been me the chalice had spoken to, I hope I would have had your courage." My jaw must have dropped. She smiled, and went out into the corridor, tucking her hands inside her sleeves.

I found Thorn in the small study on the ground floor. The room was warm, though it had large windows, to take advantage of the view of the gardens in the brief but blissful summer. Now, the fragrant bushes and arbors were blanketed with snow. He sat before the fire, his booted feet propped on the hearth, as he read from a scroll covered with runic inscriptions.

I knocked, and he turned around. Seeing it was me, he put the scroll aside, and stood. He was dressed in a white linen shirt and breeches made of deer hide, with a belt adorned with brass stars. His polished black boots matched his hair.

"Well, at last you have deigned to favor me with a visit. Or, wait. For a moment, I thought you were Magda Ranhubell, but you are much too pretty."

"Idiot," I said, feeling like a fool for the shyness that was stealing over me.

He took a mug from the table, and poured from a flagon of spiced mead. Handing it to me, he said, "Will you join me?"

"I think not." I moved to sit on the bench he had vacated. "A priestess does not drink for pleasure, remember?"

"So I have heard," said Thorn. He eyed me carefully, then sat down next to me, sipped his mead, and stared into the fire.

"Have you thought over my proposal?" he asked, gazing at me steadily.

"Yes," I said. "Tonight I spoke with the High Priestess about my calling, and she agreed."

"So, that's it," he said. He stared at me sadly, and his eyes were the same deep blue of the fjord at midnight.

I took a deep breath. "I have considered what is best for you, too, Thorn. After all, you are a magician, and a wife is a terrible burden."

His gaze did not waver.

I spread my hands. "But, if you would have an outlaw ..."

He beamed. Grabbing me to him, he held me as if I were a bird that might fly away. My whole body trembled from my hair to my heels, and I wished that he would never let me go.

I knew then that my wildness was a thing that I would give into his keeping. And he would give his wildness to me. We were each other's Keeper. I felt a new thrill, as an inkling of my destiny occurred to me at last.

"Thorn, I think I understand what magic is."

He regarded me steadily. "Yes?"

I leaned against him. "When we held the chalice, and when we shape-shifted—I as a reindeer, you as an owl—we were part of the Mother Herself ... and if there are worlds beyond, we dwelt in those too."

Thorn chuckled. "You sound just like a magician."

"But, do you see?" I said. "The power was inside us all along. The Keeper, the Goddess, the chalice—they were only trying to make us use it."

"And so we will," he said, before he kissed me with a magic that was all his own.

ABOUT THE AUTHOR

Stirling Davenport is the author of "The Nightwing's Quest,"
a fantasy novel about dark elves, and "Amphibious
Dreamers," a multi-genre collection of short stories. When
it comes to fantasy, Stirling says, "The world of the
imagination is my favorite country. It has no borders, and
no requirements for entry other than an open mind."
Stirling lives in upstate New York where she paints, writes,
and studies classical Tibetan language.